The Act: Volume II, The Circus of Women Trilogy

Volume II, The Circus of Women Trilogy

Nicole Waggoner

ISBN: 154486745X
ISBN 13: 9781544867458

For Noah and Maya and mothers everywhere.

"Making the decision to have a child is momentous. It is to decide forever
to have your heart go walking around outside your body."

—Elizabeth Stone

Ellie

Ellie's heels sank into the wet sod of the cemetery as droplets of London's signature rain fell from the overhanging branches. Regardless of how much she'd prepared herself, seeing his name on the tombstone was still a shock.

"Are you sure you're okay? You're ghost white."

"Yes." She pressed her lips into a tight line and nodded. "It's the name. Seeing it on the stone threw me for a second."

"Me, too," the answer was soft and laced with fresh pain as Pat looked up at her from his wheelchair and slipped his arm around her waist. "He was a great man."

"And so is his grandson." Ellie tore her eyes from the letters carved into the marble and squeezed his hand.

"Let's just say he's working on it." Pat smiled somberly at the grave. "Happy birthday, Pops."

Ellie took the flowers, the newspaper, and the can of Guinness from Pat's lap and gently arranged them in front of Patrick Grayson Sr.'s headstone. As she knelt, she gave silent thanks that the man she loved was still living the dash between birth and death that would one day be carved in stone.

Norah

"Yes, I have a witness."

"A witness who can solidly testify you did not examine this woman?"

"Yes." Norah checked the clock above the gate, knowing she had less than ten minutes before she boarded her flight to meet Matt for what would likely be a weekend from hell. "My NP was in the room. I told Mrs. Orlando that after a careful review of her chart, I was not the proper physician to treat her. I told her she could pick from the other doctors in the practice or we could provide her with the name of another office that accepted her insurance."

"If she follows through and sues you, I suggest you prepare to settle out of court."

"Do you understand that I never lifted the drape?"

"Yes. I do. And, frankly, I believe you were set up. That aside, do you understand that lawsuits of this nature are career-enders?"

"Yes." Norah said, thinking her lawyer didn't know the half of what was really at stake for her.

Leila

"It wasn't exactly a planned trip." Leila willed the clock to move faster. This was, quite possibly, worse than watching the minutes tick by on the elliptical at the gym.

"You expect us to believe that you ended up on a private plane by accident?" Tanya snarled and crossed her arms. "You ain't that rich."

"No. It wasn't an accident." Leila admitted and the young Hospice counselor scribbled a note on the white legal pad in his lap.

"See how she does?" Leila's mom coughed and took a long draw from her oxygen. "It don't matter what it is. She's always got something more important than family. This one takes the cake though. Running off to New York just because your friend's movie star boyfriend gets shot in the back?"

"How much planning did that take? You need notice a week ahead of time to take mamma to the doctor." Tanya took their mother's hand.

"Let's get back on subject." The counselor tapped his pen on his knee. "Tanya, from what I'm hearing, your chief complaint is that Leila committed to taking your mother to an appointment, then failed to keep her commitment because she didn't get back from her trip in time."

"Yes. Leila failed the very first time I was supposed to trust her to do anything."

The words *Leila failed* sliced through her heart like a knife.

"I take issue with the way you're framing the entire incident. I did leave town quickly and unexpectedly. I know that seems like the antithesis of everything I've said to you regarding my schedule and need to plan for the girls' care in advance. I can't go into the details of what landed me on that plane the night Patrick Grayson was shot." She looked at the counselor as if he might be able to understand her situation better than Tanya or her mother could. "I *legally* cannot. I signed an NDA."

"Well, ain't you fancy." Her mother wheezed and Leila told herself to ignore the insult.

"What I can say is that I made arrangements for my mother to get to the doctor the second it was clear that I wouldn't be back in time and contacted Tanya forty-eight hours in advance to explain the situation. She wasn't happy, understandably so, but agreed a person I knew and trusted would be better than a cab or car service."

"Then she sent some lady mamma's never met who wouldn't even let her smoke in her car."

"Don't minimalize this, Tanya. I sent a woman I consider a sister who would do anything to help me. Kate knew exactly why I had to go with Ellie and wanted to support us both. Not getting in the car was our mother's decision. When she called, railing about Kate not letting her smoke, I offered to send a cab."

"And I told you I didn't want to take no cab. They won't come to the back line of trailers and I can't walk to the front dragging this damned air tank."

"They will for medical cases. I checked with the supervisor and requested a driver familiar with that park," Leila grimaced and tried retract the words. "With that mobile home community."

"You gonna send our groceries for next week in a cab too? All that *organizing* and I still had to leave work early and lose half a shift's pay to take mamma! You can't even imagine how mad my boss was or what he said to me! You ain't the only one with kids to feed you know."

"Let me stop you there, ladies." The counselor interrupted. "I have an assignment for each of you before our next session," he looked at them sternly in turn, "and I want you to take it seriously."

Cami

Cami stood silently in the entryway of the Life After Love apartment and watched Zac stock the refrigerator. For a second, she imagined she was coming home and he was planning a meal for her. Tempting thoughts of how easy life could be with him whispered through her mind and she chastised herself for the millionth time about the one night they spent together after Blane's sister, Gracie's, wedding.

"Hi," Zac looked up from the list in his hand and stood. The flush she always felt near him crept into her cheeks and she forbid herself from noticing the way his muscles rippled as he stood. Maybe he was swimming again? Although he'd been a collegiate champion and beach guard before Blane's accident, she knew he hadn't swum since that horrific day.

"I didn't hear you come in."

"Are you, um, swimming again?" The blunt question hung in the air for a long moment before he answered.

"Yeah. I took it back up a few weeks ago."

"A few weeks ago?" She winced at the significance of that timeframe as everything she didn't want to remember about their night together came flashing back. She thought she'd imagined the taste of salt on his skin out of guilt. Had he been in the ocean that day?

"There was, um, a saltwater pool in my hotel at Gracie's wedding and I decided it was time. I don't touch the ocean anymore."

"Of course."

Cami shuddered, feeling like she was staring into her own personal wave. She'd been so stupid to lose her head with him. Stupider still to tell him she thought about him every day, sometimes in the same thought as Blane. She'd said the words organically, without thinking, when he found her on the bleachers of the track field after the reception. Sitting through Gracie's wedding and lighting the candle in Blane's memory had been torture. Every flicker of the flame spotlighted what she would never have. Cami remembered her quick goodbye to Carolyn and discreet exit after the toasts. She had driven to the high school track he loved on autopilot. She could still feel the sting of the cold bleachers cutting through the satin of her dress as she stared out over the chalked lanes. She remembered the sound of Zac's dress shoes rattling the metal and a mumbled justification for being there as he walked past her and somberly tossed a rose from the bridal bouquet out onto the clay. They sat in silence for a while before he slipped off his suit jacket and put it around her shoulders.

"I'm fine." She rubbed the bumps dotting her arms.

"Don't be stubborn. You're shivering."

"Did Gracie send you?" Cami asked quietly as the warmth of the jacket's silk lining soothed her chilled skin and a waft of his cologne, the same he and Blane had worn in college, hit her nose.

"No," he said, knitting his fingers together between his knees. "I did the same thing after Allie's wedding. He always said he grew up on this track. That it made him who he was. I guess I'm trying to give him a part of today."

"He would have been so happy for her." Cami sighed. "Did you know this was the first place he brought me when I came to meet his parents?"

"I did."

Zac's eyes seemed to follow the glow of the field lights past the stars on the horizon and into the heavens. Cami hated feeling drawn to his strong chin and mocha brown eyes.

"He was so nervous they would scare you off."

"They definitely came on strong," she laughed, thinking about how excited they were to meet *the one* as Gerry kept calling her. "But, I liked them immediately and I rarely like anyone."

"They are who they are." Zac shook his head like he was waking from a daydream. "And hard not to love." A few minutes of silence passed before he turned to her, his face serious. "Which is why I asked for their blessing before I came here tonight."

"Their what?"

He took her hand and her heart raced like she was being chased.

"Zac, no. We can't."

"Hear me out. Please."

She pulled her hand away and stared into his pleading eyes.

"I'm in love with you, Cami. In a way, I think I always was. That's why it's never worked for me with anyone else. No one will ever be better for you than me. You have to see that. I'm just asking you for a chance to love you like he would have wanted you to be loved."

The first kiss was the worst. She was speechless and reeling from the words he'd just said. She'd pulled away initially, but something deep inside of her snapped, and she opened her lips, splintering into the warmth with tears streaming down her face. For a moment, she felt whole again. Zac's need for her and the musk of Blane's cologne dizzied her head. Kissing him was wholly different than the sprinkling of casual lovers she had taken over the years since Blane's death. It held forbidden potential and stirred feelings she thought she had buried with the love of her life.

"Let me walk you out?" Zac said, bringing her back to the moment at hand and gesturing toward the apartment door.

"I didn't know you would be here. I just came to drop these off," she held up the welcome letter and envelope of expense cheques in her hand.

"And you've done that," he smiled. "Walk with me?"

"I can't, I," her eyes darted nervously around the apartment. "It's not righ—."

"It's not anything, Cami." He took a step closer. "Just a walk. Let me walk you to your car. Please? I want to talk to you."

"A walk. That's it. Don't ask me to dinner. Don't pry into my life and don't mention the wedding." A glimmer of hope crossed his face and Cami narrowed her eyes. "Because I never want to think about it again."

Kate

Kate looked into Leila's red eyes, wishing she had the right words to say.

"Are you sure you didn't agree to see the counselor with them as some sort of penance for escaping that life?"

"I don't know. I look at Tanya and I see why she resents me so much and how much more I could have done to help her. She is the youngest of my half-siblings and always had the most potential. We were never very close, mind you, partly because she turned a blind eye to everything Ronnie did to me and my mother, and partly because I spent as much time as possible out of his house. I was a college freshman when she had her first baby."

"So you were eighteen and living hours away with no vehicle." Kate said flatly, hoping her perspective would hit home.

"I could have at least offered to help her get her G.E.D. I leave those sessions feeling like the most selfish person in the world."

"That's why I'm worried."

"I know you are. So is Wes. I'm a ball of stress lately. It's like I'm caught in a loop of my failures, present and past, and running out of time to fix any of them. It's beginning to look like I'll never make things right with my mom before it's too late. I am nowhere near as prepped as

I'd like to be for my return to the university. My time at home with the girls is slipping away in a blur of tested patience and I can't seem to carve out an extra waking hour to work on any of it, much less tell you where the last month has gone."

"Leila, you're not failing. Period. You're doing the best you can in the face of what you can't control. As for the last month, give yourself some grace. You spent a week in the hospital with Ellie on top of everything else."

"I'm still not quite sure how that all unfolded, but I'm glad I was there. It was," she paused, "awful seeing her like that."

"I know." Kate shivered at the memory of watching Ellie plummet from euphoria into anguish on the night of the *Life of Us* premiere. "I'll never forget her face when it happened."

"Neither will I. It was like that famous painting...I forget the name, but it's a depiction of a man on a bridge and he's clutching his face, mouth open, looking absolutely tortured."

"The Scream." Kate said as her phone beeped. "It's called The Scream. It's my mother's favorite."

"I could see that." Leila smiled and exhaled. "Speaking of which, I never got to ask you how visiting Cameron with your mom and grandmother went."

"As expected." Kate tried to hide her pain behind a smile and a shrug of her shoulders.

"So it was awful?"

"Pretty much. Think bedpan-thrown-against-the-wall- when-the-nurse-announced-us awful." Kate forced herself to chew some salad before adding, "And it got worse from there."

"I'm so sorry." Leila put her hand over Kate's. "But you have to know his reaction is to them, not you. Right? He doesn't have quote un-quote *episodes* when you visit alone."

"I know." Kate said quietly, sinking into the maternal charm of Leila's touch. "This," she pulled her friend's hand to her knee, "is why Ellie wanted you with her. This is why she wouldn't let go of your hand when the car stopped on the tarmac. She knew you would be there for her, no matter what. She knew you could see her at her worst and love her more."

"I'm flattered that you would characterize me that way, but I think she was in shock and my going along was little more than a happy accident."

"Seriously?" Kate blanched at Leila's inability to take a compliment. "Can you give me even one example of when Ellie has been less than intentional during a crisis? I'm saying this because I'm terrified the counseling sessions you're—" Kate searched frantically for the right word—"*enduring* will re-define the way you see your commitment to the people you love."

"I needed to hear that." Leila said, looking quietly off into space as Kate's phone beeped again.

1 New Text: Cami Cell

I saw Zac at one of the LAL apartments tonight. It was an accidental run-in so why do I feel terrible?

"I mean it, Leila." Kate read the screen and wished they all, herself included, were better at forgiving themselves.

Norah

Norah took a deep breath as the car wound its way through the sprawling suburban neighborhood. One ranch style house after another passed her window until they came to a stop in the driveway of Matt's childhood home. An elderly neighbor watering his lawn looked up quizzically and Matt gave him a friendly wave.

"So we're on the same page?" he said, taking the key out of the ignition and re-adjusting his father's mirrors.

"Yes." Norah unbuckled and wiped the smudge of Matt's fingerprint from the mirror's edge with her sleeve, dreading the next forty-eight hours. "We get through the weekend and then we can make decisions when we get home." Her last word struck the tension between them like a gong. "Or, back to LA rather."

"We can do this." He gripped the wheel and shut his eyes for a moment.

"Agreed."

They opened their doors. Matt unloaded her suitcase from the trunk, carefully smoothing the wrinkles out of the yellowed plastic liner that had protected the well-used space since he was a boy. They walked in silence to the front porch. Inches before the door, she reached for his hand and he jerked away.

"I'm sorry," she whispered. "That just felt like the natural thing to do for a second."

"An act, Norah. That's all I want from you this weekend. Smile for the picture, don't piss anyone off, and save me from explanations I'm not ready to give."

Norah stared blankly at him as the realization that she was being used hit home. He was about to speak again when the front door swung open and her father-in-law, Steve, greeted them boisterously from the other side.

"Are you two coming in or what?" He held the door and shot a glance behind him as they entered. "Did you bring 'er home in one piece, or should I go count taillights?"

"She's perfect, Dad." Matt tossed him the keys as laughter erupted from the den.

"We'll see about that." Steve cracked his knuckles before heading out the door toward the car. Matt found Norah's eyes and for a fleeting moment they both wordlessly agreed that his father's affections were sorely misplaced.

"I guess I'll just put this in my room," he muttered, rolling his eyes along with the wheels of the suitcase.

Norah turned toward the den where her mother-in-law, Brenda, and Matt's sister, Faith, sat on a loveseat chatting with two women she didn't recognize. His niece and another girl lay on the floor coloring.

"Happy Anniversary, Brenda. You must be so proud." Norah smiled at her, then nodded at Faith and the other women. "You're looking well, Faith."

"Yes, yes. Come in and sit." Brenda pointed at an armchair beside the sofa. "Say hello to Phyllis, and her daughter, Barb."

"Hello," Norah shook her hand while Barb and Faith exchanged a knowing look. "It's nice to meet you both."

"You too."

Phyllis took her in as if she were a curiosity in a circus sideshow. *Step right up folks! See the woman you've heard so much about with your own two eyes! She works! She doesn't cook! She is BARREN!* Norah pushed the sarcasm from her mind and angled her chair toward their conversation.

"I've heard so much about you, Norah. Or should I call you Dr. Merrit?" Barb chuckled.

"Norah, of course."

"We missed you at the shower." Faith's voice dripped with forced geniality as she rubbed her swollen belly. "We weren't *expecting* you necessarily, but since you never RSVP'd," she shrugged her shoulders and her voice trailed off.

"I apologize. That was an oversight on my part." Norah acknowledged, trying to remember if she'd actually seen the invitation.

"It's okay, dear." Brenda raised her coffee mug to her lips. "You were probably working anyway. Matt tells us you haven't been home at all lately."

"That's true," Norah kept the smile on her face, not sure if they were digging harder than usual or if she was just extra sensitive.

"Who's your favorite princess, Aunt Norah?" Faith's oldest daughter, Kaitlin, asked looking up from the rug. Norah smiled down at her, welcoming the distraction.

"Ummm, Princess Diana.'

"Huh?" Kaitlin looked from Norah to her mother, and flipped through the coloring book. Faith, Barb, and Brenda laughed simultaneously.

"I think she means Disney Princesses," Faith snickered again and pushed herself off of the sofa. "She wants to color you a picture. Now, if you'll excuse me, that was about all this mommy's bladder could take." She laughed again in the direction of her friend.

"Maybe one day, you'll have a little girl and know as much as my mommy does about princesses," Barb's daughter said.

"No, she won't," Kaitlin answered with authority. "My mommy says her tummy is broken and she and Uncle Matt better try a whole lot harder if he wants to be a daddy."

Norah did not speak. Instead, she let the child's simple words hang in the air as the women layered one excuse over another to retract them.

Ellie

Ellie typed Pat's name into Google and flipped through the images on her phone. Despite having resigned her role as his lead publicist, she couldn't seem to let Jess manage his PR alone. A picture of them in the graveyard was already circulating, flanked by photos of the Holy Pearls' "archangels" wearing ski masks and kneeling in prayer on her defiled deck. The next trending images were of him crumpled like a rag doll on the red carpet with blood pulsing through his white tuxedo in maroon semi-circles. Article after article detailed how lucky he was to have survived and morbidly speculated outcomes, ranging from death to paraplegia, had the bullet entered a millimeter closer to his lung or severed his spine. She exited when an ad for a gaming app titled "Shoot Lucas Lucian" popped up on her screen depicting the iconic image of *Destiny's* opening scene in which an ashen, winged, shirtless Pat fell slowly from the heavens as an unconscious fallen angel into the crosshairs of a rifle's scope.

1 New Text: From Jess Cell

Just an FYI, I had them scratch the 'walk normally again' question. It's old news and only brings up the Destiny prequel.

Reply: To Jess Cell

Good call. Thank you. Where do we sit on the Globes' banquet?

1 New Text: From Jess Cell

I'm working on it, but I can't make any promises at the moment.

Reply: To Jess Cell

Add the question to the interview. We need the pressure.

Ellie forced a cleansing breath through her lips and exited the screen. She started to text Pat that the question he hated most had been dropped, then stopped and reminded herself that was what she paid Jess to do. She was getting ready for her own interview now. The grandfather clock on the wall chimed the hour as she reviewed the questions they would be asked one final time.

2 New Texts: From Patrick Grayson Cell

(1/2) I know being on this side of things isn't your favourite and I want say thank you again.

(2/2) Still want to balter?

The word 'balter' gave her pause as it always did and reminded her of the truths that had brought her an ocean away from her normal. She remembered steadying her face against the worst-case scenarios the surgeons had walked her and Pat's mother through before they were allowed to see him. She remembered looking at Leila and saying she didn't know what to do. How did she tell him that life as he knew it was over and there were more obstacles than they'd ever imagined, much less planned for, on the other side of this?

She would never forget balking at Leila's soothing tone when she said it wasn't her job to fix the situation and that no one expected that of her. *But, that's what I do,* she'd sobbed quietly into her friend's shoulder. *Not this time,* Leila had whispered, stroking her hair. *He's not asking for his publicist. No spin and no dancing backwards in high heels. He just needs you to be there for him.* Ellie protested again and Leila released her hand for the first time in hours. *Look at me,* she'd said. *All you have to do is be there and hold his hand. It's not about the dance. It's about the balter."* Ellie had stared at her, lost, and said she didn't know what that word meant. *I know you don't, but he will. Ask him.* Ellie had given herself a beat of a moment before pulling herself together to make the six-yard walk to his room that would change her life forever.

Reply: To Patrick Grayson Cell

Thank you. It's hard, but I'm ready. We're ready. I love you.

Ellie smiled at the grandpa-twerking-in-his-walker emoji he sent back, still not sure how laughing with him for the first time on her deck and the promises she made on the night "in" all felt like they had happened both yesterday and ten years ago at the same time.

1 New Text: From Patrick Grayson Cell

I know.

"They're calling for you, Ms. Lindsay."

Ellie snapped back to reality at the production assistant's voice and stood to follow him downstairs for the lighting check.

"Watch your step." She gestured to the intrusive platform of the chairlift on the stairs out of habit as they neared the landing.

"Thank you," he grinned. "I didn't see it earlier and almost took quite the tumble."

"You wouldn't have been the first." Ellie forced a smile and surveyed the scene below. Aside from the nurses standing against the wall, and the hot seat reserved for her, it was typical of any other on-location interview she'd ever orchestrated.

"You look gorgeous," Pat whispered as she took a seat beside him and fanned the crisp pleats of her belted teal skirt against the ivory sofa and crossed her ankles.

"Just there. Ms. Lindsay, don't move."

A flustered man barked to a production tech behind her.

"They're trying to counter the gleam of the metal on Pat's wheelchair so it doesn't reflect in Katie's lenses," the PA explained and took a step to the side.

"Of course." Pat tightened his freezing hand around hers and Ellie questioned whether or not they were actually ready for this.

Norah

"**M**aybe she can borrow something before I run out of light?" The photographer asked.

"I told Matt, Mamma! This isn't my fault!" Faith hoisted her youngest up from the ground.

"She, um, packed in a hurry." Matt looked at Norah guiltily and added, "I should have clarified."

"Yes," Norah glared at him. "When you bought the brand new black shirt you're wearing, you should have taken two seconds to text me and let me know the color scheme had changed."

"Don't blame Matthew! This shouldn't be his job!" Brenda slapped her thighs and stormed off toward the front yard.

"Mamma!" Matt, Steve Jr., and Faith called after her in unison.

"Excuse me." Norah turned her back to them and walked to the porch. The screen door squeaked loudly as she opened it and headed down the hallway to Matt's childhood bedroom. She sat on the twin bed and took her phone from her pocket.

1 New Text: To Leila Cell

Faith the Faithful continues to serve.

Reply: From Leila Cell

She never disappoints ☹ What happened?

1 New Text: To Leila Cell

She sent me a message 4 months ago saying she and Matt's brother had hired someone to take a family photo as an anniversary gift. They wanted the women and kids in black and the men in white. Plans changed @ the last min, no one told me, women are now in white, and I am apparently ruining the pic BC I have nothing to wear.

Reply: From Leila Cell

I'm sorry. I know you ordered the specific type of black shirt she wanted...no buttons, matte fabric, yadayada to make an effort. Ask them to Photoshop your lab coat in. That's white.

1 New Text: To Leila Cell

LOL. Thanks for the smile.

Norah rolled her shoulders as she walked to the adjoining bathroom. The option with the lowest risk was to bow out of the picture entirely rather than be photographed and stand out even more than she already did amongst the women pictured on Brenda's living room walls. She locked the door and turned her back to the mirror before unfastening the button of her jeans and slipping the denim and her underwear just below her hips. Norah counted the circles of brown blood, relieved she hadn't spotted more since that morning.

Cami

"Thanks, Boss!" Brandon said as the bartender handed him a can of Red Bull and a shot of amber liquid.

"You're welcome," Cami replied in his general direction as he hurried back to the group's table. Maybe she should replace the coffee pot in the break room with energy drinks and hard liquor. The ideas her young team had randomly spouted tonight were better than anything she'd seen from them in the office. She signed for the group tab, left a forty-five dollar tip, and made her way through the crowded room to say goodbye.

"Cami!" A familiar husky voice caught her ear. "I didn't know this was your scene."

"It's not." She turned around to face Marcus. "Look at you all dressed up."

"I aim to please." He smirked. "Have a drink with me?"

"I can't." Cami raised her voice over the thud of the music. "I've been babysitting all night and I'm ready for some quiet."

"Are you with them?" He pointed at the group she'd left in the corner.

"Yes."

"Then you already bought me this. I was sitting with them a little while ago when they ordered the last round."

"Like you don't owe me enough already?"

"Easy now. That cute little redhead, Sparrow, brought me over." He hooked his arm through hers and added, "I had no idea what I was in for."

"What are you doing?" Cami pulled her arm away.

"Helping your rep." He steered them toward the table. "Just go with it. They're watching and they've been joking about 'the has been photog' all night. You go home with the hottest guy in the bar and watch their attitudes change on Monday. You need cool credits to be taken seriously in their world."

"Cute logic. You can walk me to my car."

"I'll take what I can get." He grinned as they passed the staring table of young associates.

Ellie

"She's been my rock." Pat looked into Katie Couric's eyes and touched the back of Ellie's hand to his lips. "That's the only way to describe it. I'm still not sure how she managed to get to the hospital in New York before I was even out of surgery, but I'm relatively certain a magic carpet was involved."

"That's true." Ellie winked.

"The world knows how you met, how you fell in love," she raised an eyebrow, "and about the notes you left on Ellison's stairs. What we don't know is what happened after the red carpet. Can you tell me more about the hours between the shooting and seeing each other again?"

"I can't say I remember everything." Pat ran his hand through his hair then took Ellie's again. "It's odd because tiny pieces keep coming back to me at the strangest moments." He paused and Ellie nodded cautiously, not knowing what he would say. "Just now, for instance, I recall being in the ambulance and an EMT asking if I was allergic to anything when he slipped an oxygen mask over my face. I said 'yes, bullets,' and he made a note before he realized I was joking."

Katie laughed and Ellie shook her head, surprised again that he could make her feel relaxed even in the tensest moments.

"You're quite the character, Pat. Does he make you laugh, Ellison?"

"Yes." She allowed the flush she felt to reach her cheeks for the camera's benefit. "Every single day."

"I can see that." A mic on a boom dropped just over their heads. "And what were those hours like for you, Ellison? Was there a magic carpet?"

"Something like that. Another client my firm represents had a private plane waiting to leave LAX for New York and agreed to a hitchhiker."

"Would you care to say whose plane it was?"

"Not at this time." Ellie answered with a practiced smile and moved on. "Landing and getting into the car on the tarmac in NYC all run together in my memory, but I'll never forget the monumental relief I felt when word came that the surgery was successful." Her heart pounded behind her eyes as she recited the line she had practiced.

"What were your first words to each other when you were allowed to see him?"

Pat squeezed her hand. Ellie had argued this question should be excluded on grounds that it was too personal, but they had agreed to defer to Jess. "Seeing her walk into that hospital room was like putting an ice cube onto a burn. It was pain and relief all at once. I was overjoyed she was there, but also incredibly sad that I had dragged her into such a catastrophe."

"There were so many lines in his arm that I couldn't hold his hand," Ellie added.

"So she held a finger."

Ellie could feel the affection radiating off of him.

"I told her that I loved her," he paused, "enough to let her go. I told her she would be mad to stay. I said I couldn't be what she deserved, not with months, possibly years of rehabilitation ahead of me and countless copycat maniacs lurking around every corner, waiting for an opportunity to kill us both." He tugged at the collar of his shirt as the slightest quiver entered his voice.

"He told me I deserved to dance." Ellie steeled herself against the emotion of the memory and continued. "You see, the dance is what I knew." I built my PR empire spinning backwards in high heels and sidestepping messes. I fell in love with Pat, as off limits as he was, because I realized I wasn't dancing when I was with him. I was simply myself. Just me. And that was enough." She looked to the side, away from the cameras and closed her eyes for half a moment. "So, I told him I didn't want to dance; I wanted to balter."

"Balter?" Katie cocked her head. "I don't think I know what that means."

"It's a strange British expression that means to tread or dance clumsily." Pat moved his hand to her knee. "Which I'm awfully good at, as you well know."

Katie laughed and Ellie smiled, hopeful she wouldn't use it as a segue to ask if he would walk again.

"So, I have to ask the question burning on everyone's lips."

Pat cringed and Ellie put her hand on his as Katie continued.

"What's next for the 'Golden Couple' or PatSon, as your fans call you? It's no secret that wedding rumors are running rampant."

Ellie stared harder at the host, wondering when this question had been added and why they weren't told.

"I, umm, haven't asked her yet." Pat answered, flustered. "That doesn't mean I will or I won't. I mean to say that we're, um," his eyes bounced between hers and Katie's.

"Committed," Ellie finished his sentence. "And taking it one step at a time."

"The balter." Katie concluded as a production assistant clicked a placard.

"That about does it folks!" the producer announced proudly. "The second team will be here in the morning to refine a few shots of Mr. Grayson's loft, but you won't be needed."

The shadows in the room came to life and the crew began dismantling their equipment.

"Thank you, both." Katie extended her hand. "That interview may be my new favorite. Hearing your story in person is even more touching than I imagined it would be and I sincerely wish nothing but the best for you."

"Thank you for not asking if I would walk again."

"Thank Ellie," Katie nodded and stood.

"This is me," Ellie exhaled for what felt like the first time since she had sat in this chair. "Not exactly letting go."

"And I wouldn't have you any other way," he whispered back, and the familiar surge of wanting him sent chills all over her body.

Kate

Kate moved screaming Liam onto her other hip and tossed the burning veggies around the wok. She reached for the bottle of sesame seed oil just as his fist found her earring. In a burst of searing pain, she let the bottle slip from her hand. Kate cried out and turned off the stove. Her ear throbbed in time with his screams as she stepped over the shattered glass and growing puddle of slick oil toward the kitchen table. Liam's lip trembled as she pulled him close to her chest. Kate shuddered at the droplet of warm blood that fell to her shoulder. She could not be a mom for one more second today. She couldn't, but she would.

Leila

1 New Text: From Kate Cell

I can't seem to find anything that will give Liam relief from the teething. He's miserable.

Reply: To Kate Cell

And that means mommy is too. I'm sorry friend. Hang in there and try freezing applesauce on a baby washcloth. He might gnaw on it and numb his gums.

1 New Text: From Kate Cell

Thanks. I'll try that. I can put it on my ear next. He tore out my earring while I was making dinner and it's bleeding.

Reply: To Kate Cell

Ouch! It does make you more like Van Gough. LOL.

1 New Text: From Kate Cell

We'll go with that. Thanks for the laugh ☺

*L*eila closed her screen, thinking the space between five o'clock and seven were the witching hour for young children, as she heard Wes walk through the door.

"Hi, Beautiful." His face fell as he glanced around the silent room and loosened his tie. "Damn. I was hoping to make it in time to read stories."

"It's okay." Leila's mind raced around what their evenings would be like when she returned to work.

"No. It's not, Leila." His brow creased and she wished she could pull the pain from his eyes away. "Every day," he began to pace. "Every damned day, I line things up to leave by 5:00 and every damned day something happens."

"Sit, Wes. It's okay. I know it feels like that, but you need to give yourself a break. Tomorrow, plan to leave at 4:00 and maybe you'll make it out by 5:00."

"I don't know what to do. It's like the whole place falls apart when I'm not there and no one can do anything without me holding their hands."

"It sounds like it's time for a change."

"You've got that right." He paced to the kitchen. "Tomorrow morning, I'm calling an all hands meeting for the managers and cancelling their quarterly bonuses until I see an improvement in leadership. I can't fight the forest fires and their pint-sized brush fires all at the same time."

"I know."

Leila hated seeing him this overwhelmed, but also knew there would always be another fire behind the last. That was life at the top of your field, and delegating simply wasn't in his nature.

Norah

"Isn't that your friend, Norah?" Faith held up a magazine with a picture of Ellie and Pat on the cover. "The one the kids and I met when we surprised Matt for his birthday? He took us to her beach house so they could play in the sand without any bums lurking around, right?"

Norah noticed the date and wondered if Faith had saved it for three weeks just to ask.

"Yes. She's a good friend of mine."

"Who is?" Brenda said, leering over her shoulder and taking a stack of plates from the china cabinet.

"Pat Grayson's girlfriend." Faith pointed to the picture again and stood.

Brenda pointed sternly to the chair. "Sit, Darling, sit. I don't want you on bed rest like last time. Norah can make herself useful."

Norah remembered laughing with Matt after they visited Faith and baby number three in the hospital. Her chart had hung on the wall and Norah had scanned it from the corner of her eye as Faith regaled the family with the tale of her most difficult labor yet. Her pressures and sugars had been steady, there was no note of edema, and Norah was willing to bet true bed rest was never ordered.

"Never, EVER, tell my mother!" Matt had howled on their way back to the airport. "She's done nothing for the last four weeks but play the martyr about waiting on Faith hand and foot and taking care of Christian and Kaitlin."

"We definitely don't want that," Norah said to Brenda.

"See? Doctor's orders." Brenda retorted. "Grab the bowls."

Norah took the stack and followed Brenda to the table.

"I guess I'll obey then." Faith huffed and put her feet up on the ottoman. "*Just like my brother does*," she added under her breath.

Norah stopped dead in her tracks. "Excuse me, Faith? I didn't quite catch that."

"Oh. I was just saying I hope you enjoy dinner. I had it delivered to make things easier for Mamma on her special weekend." She smiled at her mother then thumbed the cover of the magazine open. "It's Mexican."

"Sounds good." Norah turned to leave the room.

"We don't have many around here," Faith rushed on. "Or I would have ordered El Salvadorian. Matt tells me it's your preference these days."

Norah ignored Faith's stab and continued to the kitchen. Her anger at Matt grew exponentially as every moment she spent quivering beneath Enrique's beautiful brown skin thundered through her mind. She laid out her stack of dishes in their proper places on the table then ducked out onto the porch to focus on why she was here and what she wanted to save. She would not let herself get upset. Matt had told Faith to hurt her. Faith needed to feel superior. This was their rivalry, not hers. She would sit through dinner coolly, making conversation without reaction to their faces, like she were making small talk while performing any other uncomfortable procedure. Then she and Matt would have a real discussion in private, whether he wanted to hear her or not.

Ellie

Ellie shuddered watching Pat pull himself, strained and sweaty, along the padded canvas bars during the hardest third of his daily rehabilitation session. The trauma to his back muscles had healed enough to allow him to walk short distances without assistance, but doing so for any length of time was painful to the point of impossible.

"Bloody hell!" He choked out between grinding teeth and fell to his knees.

"I think that's enough for today, Mr. Grayson," the best specialist money could buy said soothingly. "Let's do some cool down work on the mat and get you to the cryogenic chamber."

Ellie knelt beside him as one of the physical therapists pushed his wheelchair to the edge of the mat behind them. She smoothed the wet curls plastered against his forehead to the side and whispered into his closed eyes. "Give it a little more time. There's no rush."

"How can you say that to me?" Pat erupted in the harshest tone she had ever heard him use and gruffly shirked away from the therapist trying to assist him into the wheelchair. "I can do it on my own!" he barked through labored breathing as his forearms struggled to force his weight backward over the hard metal base and into the chair's seat. "I don't want to give it more time, Ellie! I want what they took from me back! What they took from us! I want to get on with our goddamned lives and not be *this* anymore!" He glared from the bars to the mat to the cryogenic unit.

Ellie ignored his volume and pulled his palms to her cheeks, feeling his outstretched arms tremor with exertion. "I know you don't. You're tired. You're in pain. You're angry. You're also *alive* and moving forward every day. That's all that matters right now."

He looked up, embarrassed, and melted from furious to defeated.

"Agreed," he said. "I'm sorry I lost my head for a second."

"In the PR industry, we call that 'going full diva,' but in this case, I think you're entitled. Frankly, I'm surprised it took you so long." She kissed him softly and stepped to the side so the therapist could push him over to the mats where the rest of the team waited.

"Let's get out tonight." He flashed a pained grin over his shoulder. "I want to show you more of my London."

"I'd love to."

Ellie felt grateful that being in public together was finally becoming bearable. The leeches still followed them everywhere, but their present intensity was mild compared to the smothering onslaught it had been just after his return to England.

As Pat finished his session and left with a nurse to shower and change, Ellie checked her messages and reviewed the agenda for a conference call she'd scheduled with her New York office. He reemerged twenty minutes later in fresh clothes and brighter spirits. Security swept the street exit of the facility and guided them to the car. Three photographers lounged lazily against the brick wall across the street and snapped a few shots. Unless he stood and fell, photos and video of them leaving rehab were old news and had lost their value.

"Give her bum a squeeze!" one shouted as the nurse bent over and helped him transfer from the chair to the car.

Ignoring them, Pat thanked her and Dominic as he always did before shutting the door. He smiled at Ellie and pressed the button to raise the privacy screen between the front and back seats.

"I made a few calls of my own while you were working," he said with a touch of mischief that reassured her he wasn't faking a better mood for her sake. "Tonight's all laid out."

"Oh? Where are we going?"

"It's a surprise." He put his hand on her knee and fondled the hem of her skirt. "Dress to impress." He walked his fingers beneath the fabric. "And bring sensible shoes for after."

The muscles in her groin clenched in anticipation as she made a note to have something evening worthy sent over from Harrods.

Kate

"Look, Ken!" Kate bolted up from her nest of pillows and handed him her phone.

"What is it?" His brow furrowed as he squinted at the blue glow of the Facebook feed.

"It's Cami. She's out with Marcus for God only knows what reason."

"Whoa." Ken blinked at the picture of the two leaving a downtown bar. "Ellie's going to freak."

"Did you see the caption? 'Caught! While the cat's away, the mice will play!'" Kate read *Hello!* Magazine's post again before closing the app. "They're citing Marcus as Example A of Ellie's taste in younger men and calling Cami her former BFF."

"It could be a good thing," Ken shrugged. "That whole triangle is bizarre. First, Marcus steals information from Ellie's client files and she's fired from Camelot. She throws him—literally—out on the street and puts a kill order on his career. The next thing we know, she's back from Cinque Terre and has hired him as a personal trainer? I always wondered what Cami thought about the whole ordeal."

"I know." Kate sank deeper into the pillow and he put his arm around her. "The funny thing is, I don't think Cami thinks much about it at all."

Ken grinned down at her and she felt a surge of anxiety at what was coming. She didn't want to rush it. She wanted to talk more first. His hand inched under the strap of her nightgown, working it off of her shoulder. Kate gave him a tight smile and moved it back.

"Cami fired him point blank when Ellie told us what he'd done, then re-hired him when Ellie did. I still don't know why."

"Well, we all know Ellie likes to be in control of every situation." He stroked her hair and lingered over her ear.

"That's true, but there's more to the story. I don't know what it is exactly, but I know it goes deeper. Cami's lips are sealed, but I asked Ellie once." She dipped her shoulder to let the thin strap fall, happy that he seemed content to slow the pace and enjoying the stir of desire budding low in her belly.

"Did she answer you?" Ken kissed the bare skin of her collarbone and slid his finger beneath the strap on the opposite side.

"She did." Kate pressed her hips closer to his. "And I've never seen her face go to ice so quickly. Ellie said she hired him as a trainer because she liked the idea of being molded into physical perfection by someone who would never have her again."

"That's intense."

"Right?" Kate said, losing herself in the wanting emerald of his eyes. "He's always been into Cami. That's not lost on Ellie. On Cami maybe, but not Ellie. Cami thinks of him like a bratty brother. Ellie will flip when she sees them together and Cami will probably wonder why she's so upset."

"Maybe she won't see it. She is a world away and hours ahead after all." He caressed her thigh beneath the sheets and Kate shifted to her side, leaning into the motion and stifling a yawn.

"You have *met* Ellie, right?" She laughed, her eyelids growing heavier as he nuzzled her neck and moved his hand beneath the cool silk covering her breast. Kate relaxed into his touch and the warm duvet, running her hands up his back, fighting harder to pry her eyes open each time they closed, until she slipped away into the dark nothingness of sleep.

Norah

"You've outdone yourself, Faith!" Matt's father placed a hand on his daughter's shoulder. "It's almost perfect."

"Thanks, Daddy." Faith beamed, leaning into him like a housecat purring under its owner's touch. "There's just nothing I adore more than preparing a meal for the people I love. It's just so," she looked smugly at Norah, "purposeful and fulfilling."

"All three times a day?" Matt challenged.

"Yes!" Faith snipped and shot him a frigid stare.

"I'm a lucky man." Faith's husband, Scott, patted his protruding belly.

"Tell me, Matt," Faith said directly to Norah, "who cooks dinner in your house? I'm assuming it's not your wife."

"Tell us, Matty! Do you strap on the old apron and cook your woman a meal?" Steve Jr. said boisterously, slapping his knee.

"Good one, son!" Her father-in-law chuckled and circled one arm around Faith and the other around Matt. "And here I was thinking that at least one of my girls had married a doctor and would be taken care of!"

Norah watched the color rise in Matt's cheeks.

"We don't exactly starve," Matt said, rattling the ice in his tea glass at his mother for a refill.

"No thanks to you, Mr. Associate at Law!" his brother bellowed, snatching the last tortilla and offering Matt the empty basket.

"On second thought, I take that back," Steve Sr. said. "Mattie may have finally outsmarted all of us. He married a doctor."

"So did I!" Faith slapped her husband on the arm.

"Chiropractors aren't real doctors," Matt muttered aloud what Norah was thinking.

"I *REPEAT*, Mattie married a doctor and DID NOT get knocked up! Now, he just sits back and waits for 'er to bring home the bacon!"

"That he does!" His brother laughed so hard he coughed into his napkin while Faith crossed her arms defensively over her chest.

"We'll get you one of those Tupperware catalogues Faith is always pushing and you can keep that cold bacon fresher longer."

"They're quality, functional products," Brenda said with a tense smile as she re-filled the tortillas and sweet tea. "In fact, maybe I'll send some of mine home with Norah. That way, she could spend just a little time cooking on the weekend and then Matt would have dinner even on her busy work nights."

"I've never been much in the kitchen," Norah conceded. "But, I am enjoying this lovely meal." She smiled in her best effort to break the tension and took another bite of the guacamole on her plate.

"I try," Faith smirked and turned to her father. "Did you notice the music, Daddy? I made a playlist."

"Yes, baby. It's quite catchy."

"I picked the songs myself."

"So you *can* use the computer when you want to," Steve Jr. jabbed. "You should teach her to pay the bills while she's sitting around the house all day playing with the kids, Scott."

Norah felt a twinge of sadness for Faith.

"It's not like I made a website or anything!" Faith sneered at Steve Jr. "I just searched an artist based on Norah's recent tastes."

Norah looked back at her, processing, as Matt stiffened and the rest of the family exchanged confused glances.

"In Enrique," Faith narrowed her eyes at Norah and let the name hit home, "Iglesias."

"What the fuck, Faith!" Matt shouted.

"Matthew!" Brenda gasped pointing to the den where the kids were eating on TV trays, engrossed in a VeggieTales movie.

"What did I do, Daddy?" Faith asked, staring doe-eyed at her father.

"You know exactly what you've done, Faith." Norah stood and backed away from the table. "You both do. Excuse me."

She took a few calm steps then stopped, burning from the humiliation burning in her chest. She turned back to the table and forced her voice to stay steady.

"Just so we're clear. I have been nothing but cordial to this family from day one. I can't say that I am the same person you hated then, but I can say that I am a better one. I have loved Matt, I have sacrificed for him, and I have suffered through more than I care to share with you for him. I will not, however, pretend with him anymore. I cheated. So did he. And it's over."

Their jaws hung open as she left the room with the echoes of everything else she wanted to say to them ringing in her head.

Ellie

"You look…" Pat blushed and wobbled a bit on his cane. "Spectacular."

"Thank you." Ellie grinned, both admiring and despising the effort it took for him to stand as he waited for her. The crushed emerald fabric of her dress hugged her hips as she walked down the remaining stairs toward him. She hurried to his side as fast as his pride would allow and caressed his cheek, loving the softness of his freshly shaved skin and the light scent of aftershave that tickled her nose.

"Truly spectacular."

"I tried," she whispered and guided him down to his chair, never taking her eyes from his. "Thank you for standing while you waited. I know it wasn't easy."

"What's easiest is not always what's right." He ran his thumb over her hand. "And I want to be—no, I will be the man you deserve."

You already are.

Ellie didn't say it, knowing she was likely anything but the woman he deserved as she tried and failed to shake thoughts about Marcus, Cami, and the chaos ensuing in the LA office from her mind. He pulled her into his lap and parted his lips to kiss her.

"Woooo-Eeee!" The nurse's happy whistle interrupted. "Don't you look smashing!"

"Thank you, Emma." Pat replied routinely and Ellie hated that they were never really alone even in private. "We've quite the evening planned." He smiled at Ellie and drew a long breath.

Leila

L eila stared blankly at the ceiling, willing her eyes to close. Wes snored rhythmically beside her and she fought the urge to look at the clock. She had gone to bed early, at nine o'clock, but had only managed fifteen minutes of sleep. Her heart beat rapidly in her chest and she told herself to inhale peace and exhale tension. She was running on the faintest of fumes these days and trying desperately not to worry about the week ahead. She shifted to her belly, hoping a new position might help her sleep. Her mind flashed from her mother to her syllabus to the daycare newsletter to Clara's dance checklist to the dry cleaning that was overdue for pick up to sitting by Pat's bedside with Ellie after his second surgery.

He was in and out of consciousness that evening, and Ellie hadn't left his side in over ten hours. Nature called eventually and she asked Leila to hold his hand while she stepped out. Touching the fragile shell that looked like Lucas Lucien seemed surreal. She felt like she was violating some sort of trust by thinking of him that way. Even though they had never met, he would always be that sexy *Destiny* boy and her celebrity crush. Leila had all but jumped out of her skin and lost her own bladder when Pat's fingers came to life and curled around hers. His eyes had twitched violently before opening and darted around the room as he clumsily tried, but failed, to push himself to sitting. Leila winced with him in pain as the IV pulled and he lay back down, panting.

"Where's Blythe?" He'd wanted to know, slurring his words. "I need to know she's okay. Tell her I love her."

The urgency in his tone crescendoed on the last syllable as his face convulsed in pain. Leila told him Blythe wasn't there, but Ellie had just stepped out and would be back shortly. He stared at her, processing his surroundings in dizzied embarrassment.

"I'm sorry." He shook his head and squeezed his eyes tightly closed before opening them again. "I was dreaming about the premiere. About being on the carpet, just before the shooting. But it was *Destiny* because Blythe was there. She was holding my hand." His voice was raspy and parched. "Which is why I was confused seeing you. You look a bit like her."

"Me?" Leila exclaimed, an octave too high, surprised and giddy that he had compared her to someone so beautiful. "I mean that's sweet of you to say. She's so elegant and I'm just a dumpy mom of two who wears more marker than couture. I mean to say I would be an absolute mess on the carpet, tripping over my own feet and stumbling around on heels. I can barely walk across my classroom without teetering. I'm sorry to ramble," she flushed and he stared curiously at her. "We've never really met, have we? You don't even know my name! I'm Leila. Leila Oliver. It's so nice to, um, meet you. Ellie just loves you. I mean, um, well you know that. I don't work for her. She'll be right in, um, let me go get her, and a nurse, and, um, would you like some water?"

"Yes." The sly, cautious expression that had always left her wanting more Lucas Lucien crossed his face. "All of those things would be lovely."

"No problem."

She stood and walked to the sink to get him a glass. Her hand shook as she lifted the pink plastic pitcher and she told herself to get it together. Ellie would not appreciate her acting like a giddy teenager around him.

"I'm sorry. Did you want ice, or maybe prefer a bottle? I didn't think to ask before I—" she caught her toe on the edge of the IV cart. "Ouch!"

Leila cried out and the world seemed to fracture into slow-motion frames as the water flew out of the cup and onto his chest. "Oh my God!" she screeched watching his white gown turn transparent. "You'd think I never waited tables! I don't know why I'm so nervous, but I am. I've been here for a week! I mean, I'm sorry."

"Thanks," Ellie said as she opened the door talking to a nurse. "He's awake?" She stopped in her tracks.

"He is," Pat smiled at Ellie and Leila could feel the magnetic charge between them. "Your friend was just giving me a bath."

"I, um," she began apologetically. "No charge for that."

Pat had laughed, but Ellie looked confused.

"Why don't I go find a towel?"

Leila blushed at the memory and snuggled into the crook of Wes' arm. He stroked her back automatically, still snoring. She ran her hand through his thinning hair and he murmured something in between snores.

"I love you," she whispered wanting to wake him for sex, but hesitant because they'd already made love when they came to bed and because he had to be up in three hours. He stirred beneath her touch and she thanked God again for the gentle loving man she was blessed to have in her life and prayed over the growing stress lines on his forehead that he would find a better balance between work and family.

Ellie

Pristine white blossoms stretched over the braided woodwork of the conservatory's trellises for what seemed like an eternity. Mirror upon mirror reflected their beauty as candles flickered on each table and fairy lights hung overhead.

Ellie couldn't believe her eyes as she glanced around the empty space. "Pat, this just might be the most beautiful courtyard I have ever seen."

"I'm glad you fancy it because it's ours for the evening."

"As in alone?"

"Yes," he beamed up at her from his wheelchair.

"Mr. Grayson, Ms. Lindsay," a polished voice announced from behind them. "I am Alistair Damask and I will be taking care of you this evening. The conservatory is at your disposal for as long as you like."

"It's a pleasure to meet you, Alistair."

"The pleasure is mine, sir." He gestured with his gloved hand to a linen covered table set with gold chargers and sparkling crystal. "May I show you to your table?"

"Dominic, will you kindly lend me a hand with my cane? I'd like to walk my date to her seat." Dominic obliged, albeit with a stern shake of his head, and Pat pushed himself up from the wheelchair, smiling from ear to ear as he steadied himself on his tri-footed cane. Ellie hooked her arm through his. The table was only a few hundred feet from them, but it might as well have been a mile.

"Mind the pavers, Mr. Grayson," Alistair said genially, pointing to the stone floor as Pat put one foot in front of the other.

Dominic followed two feet behind them, ready to catch Pat if he fell. Another security guard stood on the opposite wall, arms crossed and looking like a suited sentinel.

"I understand this is your first time at Clos Maggiore, Ms. Lindsay?"

"It is." Ellie answered absently, worrying that Pat was needlessly exerting himself.

"Our menu is Provencal-inspired and the chef has prepared a special trio of caviar offerings in your honor."

Pat interrupted Alistair's reach for her chair. "Allow me."

Before this evening, Ellie had always protested that having her doors opened, meals paid for, and chairs pulled out were condescending attempts by men to control her with flattery. And, most of the time, in boardrooms, press functions, and contract negotiations, they were.

"You're blushing."

"I know." She lowered her eyes and slipped into her chair. "Your manners seem to have that effect on me."

Alistair flipped the tip of the tented silk napkin from the middle of her charger so that it fanned in the air and spread flawlessly on her lap, then excused himself after Pat was seated.

"Can it be that Ellison Lindsay, the powerhouse, likes to be courted? Shocking." Pat laughed and reached for his napkin.

"What can I say? A chair pulled by you makes me feel valued, not owned." She lifted the glass of chilled champagne in front of her place setting. "This is us."

"To us." Pat raised his goblet and took a sip before blotting his brow with a crisply pressed handkerchief. "Growing stronger every day."

The unmistakable click of a camera's lens sounded from behind the thick hedges. Dominic gave them a thumb's up and, knowing it was being handled, Ellie took another sip of champagne and looked at the wine list. They sat in comfortable silence until Alistair reappeared with a platter of caviar. He chattered excitedly about the harvest and its rarity before slipping away to let them enjoy it.

"How does anyone truly care for this filth?" Pat asked scattering the orange orbs discreetly beneath the saffron encrusted crackers. "I was photographed choking it down at a dinner in Modesto after the first *Destiny* premiere and it's been 'gifted' to me ever since. Blythe loved it, but I always thought it tasted like feet."

"Feet?" Ellie snorted. "How do you know what feet taste like?"

"Just a wager. But be my guest if you're into that sort of thing." He grinned with a shrug as Alistair approached, scrutinizing the portion left on her plate.

"Was everything to your liking, Ms. Lindsay?"

"It was divine." Ellie said, feeling the champagne burn into her stomach.

"The chef has prepared a lovely rack of lamb for Mr. Grayson this evening and a butter poached rock lobster for Miss Lindsay. May I suggest a wine pairing? Our selection is unmatched in all of London."

"Please."

Pat winced and Ellie watched a fresh wave of pain cross his face while he agreed to Alistair's suggestions. Her phone buzzed in her clutch and she fought the urge to check it, imagining proposal rumors circulating from the pictures that had just been snapped of their elaborate date.

"Is it important?"

"No." She lifted her glass. "Not tonight."

"So, I've been waiting to ask you something."

"You can ask me anything. You know that."

"It's about the Golden Globes' banquet."

"What about it?" She cocked her head, hoping he'd changed his mind about refusing to go without her.

"Jess thinks I should go. She says it would look disrespectful of the Globe board to decline and could damage my career."

"I strongly agree."

"I've spoken to the director and to the cast and they all want me to go." He pushed a wave of auburn hair behind his ear.

"So you've changed your mind?"

"I haven't." His eyes pleaded for her approval. "I know it sounds dramatic and even a tad selfish, but I don't feel that going honors the work. You're not allowed, simply because you're a publicist, and I'm invited based on taste that is subjective at best. Meanwhile, Roland's husband and children have yet to see a cent from his benefits because their state doesn't recognize same sex marriages. I want to take a stand for them, and for Roland, against rules that discriminate and exclude."

"And that's very noble of you, Pat. I'm just not sure the Globe board is an enemy you want to make at this point in your career." She reached for his hand. "Go to the banquet. Take your mom. Marriage equality will happen in our lifetime. It's a nonissue at this point. My concern is that you are going to burn a bridge that we can't rebuild."

"We being?"

"Me, you, Jess, and the firm. Trust me when I say for the hundredth time that you do not want to snub the Globes." She brought his hand to her lips. "No spin."

"I know." He dropped his shoulders. "But it still doesn't seem right."

"Then, we ask the family. Let it be their call."

"And assuming they agree, I would go without you?"

"In theory."

She squeezed his hand as Alistair presented a bottle of reserved wine and preached its accolades before expertly pulling the cork and pouring a taste for Pat.

Norah

"**N**orah! Norah, wait! I'm sorry."

Matt flung the storm door open and rushed to the end of the driveway where she stood with her suitcase.

"You're sorry? I know you're sorry! Does it ever occur to you that those words are always on your lips? Always!"

"You have to listen to me, Norah."

He grabbed her arm and she pulled it away.

"Actually, I don't."

"I never meant for this to happen. Faith is crazy. We all know that. She's crying her eyes out in there and feels terrible."

"I'm sure she is." Norah willed her taxi to appear, picturing wounded Faith lapping up the attention she so clearly craved. "Don't you get it, Matt? I agreed to come here as a peace offering. We agreed we couldn't get the help we need if other parties—your family or my girls—were in our ears. We agreed to keep our problems private this weekend to buy ourselves some time and you violated that!"

"So I told my sister in confidence! I'm sorry! She promised not to say anything."

"And you believed her?"

"Yes." He ground his toe into the driveway. "It was stupid."

"I get that they push your buttons and pry into your personal life, but why throw me under the bus? You're a grown man with a million other things to discuss."

"Is that what you think? What am I but a second rate attorney and a doctor's husband? People don't see me. I don't matter until they see you."

The rage she had kept at bay since he brought another woman to her bed escaped the brick in her throat and she let her eyes bore into his. "See me what? See me taking care of patients for sixty hours a week and fighting traffic to get home to watch you play Xbox? *If* you're in town that is?"

"God, Norah! You're so fuckin' selfish! You never think about anyone but yourself!"

"You're wrong," she said, grateful for the shiny yellow hood approaching in her peripheral vision. "I think about everyone else except myself. You, my patients, my friends. I'm like a sled dog that mushes until it collapses. That changes today. I've bent over backwards to make you happy, and it's not enough. I'm done. Come to counseling or don't. Go carve whatever path to success you feel I'm preventing you from."

She lifted the lever of her suitcase and rolled it to the curb, wondering how many more excuses the neighbors could invent to walk into their front yards and stare at them.

"You are not seriously going to leave me here to clean up the mess you made in there, are you?"

"I'm going home, Matt. I'm going home to take care of myself and—" she clipped the words a breath too late, and accusation colored him crimson.

"And who, Norah? Him?" Matt's eyes were frantic and he reached for her arm again.

"No." Norah stepped out of his reach and realized that she hadn't said the word 'baby' aloud to anyone yet.

"Then, who? Take care of you and—" The anger on his face yielded to hope and she turned away. "Are you?"

"Yes." She kept her back to him.

"Is it mi—?"

"Likely."

She turned to face him as the cabbie stood awkwardly by the open passenger door.

"Stay. Or let me come with you."

"No. This changes nothing."

"I'd say it changes everything!" He threw his hands in the air, fists clenched.

"We are broken, Matt. This doesn't change that. I wish it did, but it doesn't. We get help and see if we can build a new life together, or we carry on separately."

"So, that's my only option? Your terms or nothing?"

"That's not what I said."

"Aren't you done groveling yet, Mattie?" Steve Jr. yelled from the front door. "Get back in here. Faith wants to serve dessert!"

"This isn't over," Matt hissed in an exasperated whisper that pierced her to the core. "Even if we are."

She watched him walk away, ordered her lungs to breathe, and opened the door to the cab.

Cami

1 New Group Text: To SisterFriends

I was photographed with Marcus tonight. It was innocent. I wanted you to hear it from me before you see it somewhere else.

Cami pressed send and watched the minutes tick by on the treadmill in her home office. She increased the speed to full sprint, hating how violated she felt by what the camera's lens had fabricated. It would be one thing if she'd done anything wrong, she thought, raising the incline as Marcus' words raced through her head with every rotation of the belt.

"I need you to know I didn't plan this. I really didn't. The cameras just show up now. It's the whole Ellie and Patrick Grayson thing. Every magazine in town wants to know what I know about her. "

"I don't believe you."

It was the last thing she had said to him before getting into her car amidst a barrage of flashing bulbs. He had knocked on her window until she rolled it down.

"What else could you possibly have to say?"

"To quote our friend," he grinned. "There's something else you need to know. Let me in."

"Text me," she had all but spit at him, and punched the button to roll the window up.

Less than ten minutes later, he messaged that he was accepting a deal to be part of an *US Daily* spread that read *Beauty, Power, and Boy Toys! Some Women Have it All!* He was being featured as Ellie's private masseuse in addition to her personal trainer and was quoted saying she enjoyed a happy ending after each session. Although he swore his words had been twisted, Cami knew he would leap at the chance, not only for fame but to financially escape from the contract he had stupidly signed with Ellie. She took her phone from the dock and replied to his message.

Reply: To Marcus Cell

Masseuse? Happy Ending? If they print that BS, u better run and hide.

1 New Text: From Marcus Cell

I plan 2. In Cancun. Wanna come?

Reply: To Marcus Cell

This isn't a joke. You lied and people will get hurt.

1 New Text: From Marcus Cell

She can afford it. So can he.

But I can't. Cami began her cool down stride, certain that this fiasco was karmic retribution for her night with Zac after the wedding. She had used a good man who deserved better and now she was being used in return.

Reply: To Marcus Cell

You're fired.

Cami wiped the sweat from her brow. Her phone beeped with an incoming call from Marcus and she silenced it, pulling up the group message she had sent to the girls instead.

1 New Group Text: To SisterFriends

Also, I've slept with someone inappropriate and I hate myself for it. It wasn't Marcus. That's ridiculous. Ellie, I owe you an explanation.

Cami shut down her phone in favor of a shower, knowing there was little to no hope she would sleep tonight despite the run.

Ellie

"**T**here's no one here but us? How did you possibly—"
Ellie marveled at the hundreds of empty chairs in the auditorium, feeling like she was walking through a dream. In the space of an hour, they had gone from a decadent pot de crème at Clos Maggiore to the OmniMax Planetarium at the Natural History Museum.

"Let's just say I am a loyal donor."

"It's breathtaking," she said, more to the intricate maze of stars on the domed ceiling than to Pat.

"Want to show me Orion?" he grinned, all dimples, at his own allusion to her adolescent angst. Of the evenings they had spent together, their night of confessions on the pallet under the skylight was still her favorite. "Or better yet, maybe I'll show you."

"I think starry nights are becoming our constant." She took his hand from the wheel of his chair, enthralled by the tingle that spread over her skin and the twinkling beauty surrounding her. On second thought, maybe that tingle was their constant.

"Sit with me?"

"Always." She lowered herself to the side of his lap as gingerly as possible.

"I'm not made of glass you know." He raised a thigh so that her weight shifted to the center.

"Part of you is. For the moment anyway." Ellie cupped his smooth cheek in her hand and brushed his lips with hers.

"Do you remember the first time I said *this is us* to you?"

"Of course."

"I worried then that being with me would deprive you of the most basic things. When you touch me as if I'm seconds away from crumbling like an eggshell, I worry that the worst version of that fear has come true."

"Pat, I'm being cautious because I'm terrified of hurting you."

"Trust me when I say you won't." He tucked her head into his shoulder and wheeled them far too fast to the middle of the long ramp that led to the floor of the auditorium. "I never worry about that. Present vulnerabilities included. I want you to feel how much I trust you, Ellie. I've only trusted one other woman like this before."

"Your mom?" Ellie teased, knowing he meant Blythe, even though she had hurt him terribly in the end.

The corners of his mouth turned up into a smile and she made a mental note to get Blythe on board with convincing him to attend the Globe Awards' banquet. It might be unprofessional to ask a personal favor of a client, but she felt loving him included protecting him from endangering any chance he had at being recognized for serious film.

"Your trust means the world to me, Pat. In fact, I think I love myself a bit more because of it. I can't explain why exactly, but it's as if you see the person I'm meant to be. When I see myself through your eyes, I know who I am at my core and what I deserve." She kissed his neck, surprised at the sudden lock of the wheels below them.

"Ellie," he searched her eyes with a new tenderness that made her hold her breath. "Everything else tonight, what's been before—the oleander, these stars—and what I hope will come later, pales in comparison to the words you just said."

The pad of his thumb slipped to her cheek and across her bottom lip. Ellie melded into him, her body begging to respond physically to the warmth filling her soul.

"I could hold you like this all night," he murmured and pulled a few inches away. "But, I thought we might have a lie down before we turn into pumpkins and Dominic drags us out of here."

Pat flashed his most convincing smile beyond the end of the ramp to where a pillowing white duvet sat surrounded by flickering electric candles.

"You recreated the pallet?"

"Let's go see how I did. If you don't mind helping me up, that is."

"Are you sure? It's steep."

"Steep and well worth it."

"You have to tell me if the incline is too much."

Ellie unstrapped his cane from the chair back and slipped her shoulder beneath his as she had done so many times during her sister's weakest days and so many times since he had left the hospital. He tested his footing and then placed his full weight on the cane. She could sense his muscles pulsing in exertion with every step until, at last, they were at the pallet beneath a map of glimmering constellations.

"I, um," he stumbled over his words as he knelt to the white duvet and she knew he was stalling to catch his breath. "I thought we might get comfortable and see what we see."

Pat pointed to the ceiling, shrugging his sport coat to the floor and unfastening the top two buttons on his shirt. Ellie slipped off her shoes and sat beside him, tucking her legs to the side and shimmying into his open arms. He kissed her with an urgency that made her wish they were alone, not waiting to be interrupted, and gently guided her down onto her back. Ellie mirrored the motion of his mouth, distracted and trying to locate security on the perimeters.

"They're outside the main doors," he whispered, caressing her thigh. "We're alone." His other hand slid under her hair. "And the security cameras aren't on."

"Pat—we—can'tuuh," Ellie protested as her nipples hardened at his lips on the base of her jaw, straining the fabric of her bra along with her resolve.

Despite the doctors' strict orders for pelvic celibacy until his injuries were fully healed, she'd been anything but deprived since they arrived in

London for cryotherapy. Ellie knew it shouldn't matter, but she always felt a surge of relief seeing his naked hardness as his hands played her body like a piano. Every time, the darkest corners of her mind questioned whether or not her relief that he hadn't been left impotent was a glaring red flag that she was incapable of loving anyone unconditionally.

"But we can," he whispered elongating the words in a trail from her neck to her ear. "I had a call from Dr. Havens. Scans and films were good. We're clear to try." He took her earlobe between his lips and her groin clenched in desire. "I am game to go home whenever you are."

Leila

"Thank you for coming early," the young counselor said.

Leila took her seat in the hard plastic chair, smoothing her yoga pants as if they were a skirt. She had intended to wear something more appropriate for an appointment with a professional, but the insanity of the morning left her no time to do so. She would find a way to get "work ready" hair and makeup by six instead of her usual seven-thirty before her classes began.

"You're welcome." She smiled politely, hoping he hadn't noticed that she'd just smoothed an imaginary skirt.

"I asked you to come early so we could discuss the assignment I gave you. I thought you might feel more comfortable without Darla and Tanya."

"I appreciate your consideration." Leila shifted in her seat, wondering if he thought she was doing a horrible job of communicating when they were in the room.

"Let's start with the question. I asked you to catalogue the times you felt completely safe and cared for. I want to focus on instances when someone else was not only in control, but had your needs as priority one and met them as such."

"I've definitely given it a lot of thought," she answered, reminding herself not to fidget. "Sadly, my list is very short."

"Understandable. Let's start with the first moment that came to mind."

"My oldest daughter, Clara, was two-and-a-half weeks old and I was exhausted. She was nursing every twenty minutes, around the clock. Every feeding was toe-curling torture when she latched, then she would stop suddenly and we would have to start over. I also bruised my tailbone during delivery so sitting, standing, and lying down were equally unbearable." Leila forced a nervous laugh into his passive face. "Those were my zombie days. I felt like I was stumbling through a fog sunrise to sunset, half-awake, in someone else's body." Her humor fell flat and she wondered if a female counselor would be more empathetic.

"I'm hearing that you were in pain and overwhelmed. Is that correct?"

"Yes." Leila looked down at her laced fingers and ran her right thumbnail over the cuticle of her left thumb. "And alone. Wes, my husband, was only able to be with me for the first two days after we brought Clara home from the hospital. It was just me and the baby from 5:00 AM to 7:00 PM, if not later. There were visitors, of course, and friends who brought us food, but I was so embarrassed by the messy state of my house and how disgusting I felt in my red-eyed, unshowered state that I spent the visits rambling apologies about smelling like spit-up and reassuring them that I was adjusting easily to the parenting gig."

"What was your husband's reason for returning to work so quickly?"

"From the second we knew the due date, we knew his project would be ending and wouldn't allow him to be off for more than a few consecutive days. I realize it sounds like I am justifying his absence, but it couldn't be helped."

"Do you think his behavior was normal?"

"It was normal for Wes," she said, irritated at his implication.

"Where was your mother during that time?"

"At her home."

"Did you ask her to come?"

"Not directly. She came to the hospital the day I was released and asked if she could stay with us the following week. I agreed and thanked her, knowing she wouldn't follow through. And she didn't. She didn't see Clara again until she was six months old."

"I see. Why was such a difficult period in your life the first thing that came to mind when you read my question? What happened to make you feel safe and cared for?"

"Wes came home to me nursing Clara in the living room. I was crying happy tears because it was the first full feeding she'd taken in days and I knew it meant that I might be able to sleep for almost an hour." Leila paused at his underwhelmed face, now certain a female therapist would better understand the small victory that was that moment. "As soon as I handed her to him, the smoke alarm went off, startling her awake and she screamed. The leftovers I'd forgotten I was heating were burning in the oven. The only way I can describe that moment is one of pure and utter defeat. I was looking across the room at the two people I loved most in the world, feeling like I was failing both of them. Wes walked over and put his arms around me and we just stood there for a moment holding our wailing baby surrounded by ear-piercing noise. He kissed me on the cheek and said, 'Let's get out of here.' I soothed Clara while he turned off the alarms and tossed out the scorched lasagna. Then, he strapped her into her car seat and handed me my shoes."

"And where did you go?"

"To get some drive-thru chicken. Clara fell asleep two minutes after we left, so we ate driving in circles listening to her lullaby CD. It was my first substantial, uninterrupted, meal since before giving birth. Nothing has ever tasted so good. I fell asleep on the way home, mid-sentence. When I woke up hours later, I was covered with his jacket and my seat was reclined. It was almost two in the morning."

"So he drove all night?" The therapist cocked his head to the left.

"Yes, Clara and I were both still asleep when we made it to the drive-way, so he just kept going. Waking up, seeing him smiling over at me, feeling so warm and full, then drifting back off until she woke to feed, was cathartic in the midst of a major life change and struggling to meet my own basic needs in conjunction with my newborn daughter's needs."

"How do you think things would have been different if your mother, or Tanya, or another family member had been there to help?"

"I hope you understand I wasn't sitting around pining for my mommy; I never expected her help."

"I do hear that. I also hear that you are more upset that she wasn't there than that your husband wasn't there. Do you think she could have eased the fatigue, the visits from friends, the housework piling up, etc., if she had been?"

His words touched a nerve and Leila swallowed her temper.

"No, she wouldn't have made things easier. She would have held the baby in five-minute intervals between cigarette breaks in the backyard, embarrassed me in front of our guests, snipped at Wes, and sat glued to her soaps while I scrubbed dishes." Leila exhaled deeply and shook her head. "Maybe that's the problem. I have expectations she can't possibly meet."

The words to tell him she was a veritable orphan formed on her lips just as the clanking of a metal oxygen cart rattling over the peeling linoleum in the hallway drew closer and the stench of stale cigarettes and knock-off Chanel #5 hit her nostrils. "They're here."

Kate

Kate disconnected at the sound of Cami's voicemail and typed a text.

1 New Text: To Cami Cell

Are you ok?

Reply: From Cami Cell

Can't talk now. Yes and no. Worried what Ellie will think. Jess called asking to meet with me and their legal department in an hour.

1 New Text: To Cami Cell

Ellie will understand.

Reply: From Cami Cell

LOL.

I New Text: To Cami Cell

Just speak from the heart. You know she loves you and
probably knows more about why Marcus did this than any
of us.

Her screen stayed silent and she hoped she was right. Ellie was hyper-
sensitive about anything involving Marcus and she did not want to see
either friend hurt.

Norah

Norah sat on the edge of the bed, eerily aware that everything in the room was both different and the same all at once. These were her things, their things, but belonged to the people they used to be. She pulled her phone from her pocket and snapped a picture of the two empty suitcases that sat open on the floor.

1 New Message: To Mom Cell, Leila Cell

I left, walked out rather, before the party. His family knows about the affair. I'm home and packing until we have a direction. Where do I even start?

She attached the photo of the empty bags and pressed send.

Reply: From Mom Cell

With his things. Nothing says you have to leave.

Reply: From Leila Cell

Start with what's most important. Even if it's temporary,
you might be glad to have your photos, etc., with you.
You're welcome here if you don't want to be alone.

For a moment, Norah toyed with the idea of filling the bags with Matt's things and leaving them by the front door. She had sat in this very same spot, next to their packed bag for the World Health Organization conference in San Francisco just a few short months ago. She closed her eyes and let the memory of that argument flood her mind.

"Then I won't be needing *these* will I?" Matt had tossed his swim trunks to the floor.

"Conference schedules change, Matt. I can't help it if my presentation was bumped to mid-day instead of at the breakfast. We'll still have time for us. There's the keynote address tonight, but we can skip it and go to dinner. After that, there's a cocktail reception that I'll need to make an appearance for, and then we can go up to the room." She remembered his glare, how she'd picked the swim trunks up from the floor, folded them into a tight square, and tucked them back into the suitcase. "Look on the bright side. Now we can sleep in and order room service for breakfast. You can relax by the pool during my speech and I'll meet you at three. The rest of the day will be ours until—"

"Until?"

"Until the gala at seven-thirty that night."

"Can't you hear yourself, Norah? It's like I'm listening to f'n Ellie spin a situation." He had raised his pitch an octave higher and mocked, "Bring the trunks, Matt. You won't get to relax with your wife by the pool for more than an hour, but you will get breakfast in a hotel room. Never mind that you travel weekly and eat ninety percent of your breakfasts in hotels because room service is novel to me! See how I'm squeezing you in?"

"That's not exactly fair, Matt. You knew this was a half-work, half-vacation weekend. I'm telling you that you don't have to come to hear me speak, and that we'll still have a considerable amount of time by the pool together. Why can't a nice dinner tonight, a few glasses of good champagne at the reception, and two nights in a five-star hotel be enough?

Why are you letting one small change in the schedule ruin what could be a great weekend?"

"I'm upset because our day by the pool was the only thing that was really about us, Norah! The rest of the weekend will be all medical talk and sitting through that ridiculous gala!"

"I don't understand you right now. You bought a new jacket for the gala! You said you were looking forward to it! I get being disappointed about a day by the pool, but the gala? That's half of the reason most spouses come. It's a good time!"

"Most spouses? *Most* spouses? Insult me again, why don't you?"

"What? How is that insulting? Aren't you my spouse?"

"Can't you hear yourself, Norah? It's like you're saying 'Go sit by the pool, Mattie. I'll call you when it's arm candy time.' How am I supposed to feel right now? Should I go shopping with the wives and spend your money too? Or maybe visit the spa? As long as I'm back in time for your party, right?"

"Do *you* hear yourself? God forbid that you come watch my speech, much less show any pride in what I do, or notice that over half of the physicians in attendance are female, right? Instead, just focus on the two hours at the pool we won't have together. Look, I'm not forcing you to go. I want you to come, but not if this is going to be your attitude. There are other things at stake here."

"Believe me! I know! You never let me forget what your priorities are for a second."

"It's a medical aide conference, Matt! The connections I make this weekend will staff the fistula clinics in Mumbai. That's important too. The fact that it happens to be in a beautiful hotel in our favorite city should make it a win-win. I don't understand why it has to be all or nothing with you. We're going skiing just the two of us in a few weeks. Why can't you enjoy both trips?"

"That's not the point, Norah. The point is that I come second. Always."

"That's not true. If this were a law conference and the situation was reversed, I would be by your side supporting you."

"Well, it's not reversed is it? It's me waiting on you. At home, at work, or by the pool. It's always me waiting on you."

He chunked the swim trunks back to the floor and fire fanned into her cheeks.

"I'll do you one better," he said. "You go alone. I'd hate for you to miss a fundraising or staffing opportunity because you were spending time with me."

"That's not what I want, Matt. I want us to go together. It can still be a nice weekend."

"No, you don't. You want me to follow you around like a puppy, content with the crumbs of time you drop and the obligatory ovulation fuck."

Norah's heart rate rose as she remembered his intensity and the sinking feeling as she replaced the new lingerie in the suitcase with her favorite faded Berkley Med t-shirt. Little did she know she would sleep in Enrique's arms for the first time that very night.

She gathered a few photos, several sets of scrubs, and three outfits that passed as interchangeable. Norah looked around their room, perhaps for the final time, before carrying her suitcase downstairs to the kitchen. She took the magnetic notepad from the refrigerator and wrote

> *Matt,*
>
> *I don't know what to say except that we are both angry. You must have as many questions as I do and there are no easy answers to where we go from here. Only options. Please consider seeing a marriage counselor with me.*
>
> *Norah*

Her stomach twisted at the thought that the girl he was potentially still bringing home would read it first, so she pulled an envelope from the bill drawer, wrote his name, and stuck it to the handle of the refrigerator.

Ellie

"We're clear to try? Really?"

Ellie's heart raced with equal parts excitement and fear. "The doc made no guarantees about performance." Pat blushed.

"I'll be gentle." She kissed him again, then lay flat and stared up at the stars.

"It's in the little moments like these," his finger traced the line of her cheek, "when I forget that we're in the spotlight now."

"I know. It's like we've gone back in time to the condo and aren't lying on the ground in a public place."

"Ha. Ha. Speaking of which," he propped himself up on his elbow. "Have you made any decisions?"

"Nothing firm." She pursed her lips, recalling the police pictures of her ransacked rooms after the break-in, knowing the space would never feel the same.

"You can always stay at my place in Bel-Air." He tucked a strand of her hair behind her ear. "It seems strange you've never been there."

"I'll likely stay at the Mandarin until you arrive or until the contractors finish my place. It wouldn't feel right to invade your space like that." Ellie pressed her cheek deeper into his shoulder. "Without you being there that is. You'll be back soon after and can give me the personal tour, right?"

"I can't say I'm looking forward to returning to California any more than I am looking forward to being apart from you. I've gotten rather used to being back in London, even if the circumstances were less than ideal."

"I know." Ellie looked into his eyes, grimacing at the part of her that was anxious to get back to the office. It wasn't that she wanted to leave him, more that she wanted a clear picture of what had gone on in her absence. Her staff was being less than transparent in their reports and she suspected there were things she wasn't being told.

"Let's put that out of our heads for tonight." He kissed her ear whispering, "Right now, all I want is to whisk you home and make up for lost time."

— ∼ ∽

Ellie locked her eyes on the reflection in the beveled mirror floating above Pat's bathroom counter and smiled at the nerves fluttering in her stomach. She ran her thumb over the satin edge of the lingerie she was wearing and turned to the side, frowning at the definition she had lost in her lower obliques since leaving LA and nodding approval at the swell of her cleavage trussed up by the soft peach lace. Her hair sat high on her head in a sleek twist, still styled from earlier, and looking far too formal. Ellie pulled one bobby pin free, then another, letting the blond layers fall in soft waves onto her shoulders. The prickle in her scalp made her feel at home and reminded her of how much she would miss slipping into bed next to Pat every night when she left. With her hair down, the lace and silk reflecting back at her seemed to mock the intimacy to come instead of adding to it. Neither she nor Pat needed a reminder as to how fleeting their time together might be, she thought, and slipped the straps from her shoulders. The cool silk fell to her ankles and she stepped out of it, smiling at the gold trim of her aquamarine heels and deciding to keep them on. She stood in front of the mirror, naked except for the dip of the mesh thong. Ellie exhaled deeply, stood straighter, and opened the door. Timberlake's *Blue Ocean Floor* played softly in the background as she stepped into the room. Pat's eyes gaped and his face broke into the mischievous grin she loved.

"Wow," he mouthed as she walked to the bed.

"I could say the same to you."

Ellie watched his eyes trace her body from head to toe as she slowly slid the thong to her ankles, stepped out of it, and then reached down to remove the heels one at a time, stopping to relish the rush of anticipation in her chest as she slid over the cool gray sheets and took his lips in hers. He pulled her closer to his chest and she let her hands linger over the curve of his arms before moving her attention to the base of his throat. Pat's hands found their familiar place on her hips and Ellie slipped her legs to either side of his body deliciously lost in the moment until his grimace snapped her into the realization that she was falling into their old rhythm and forgetting that her weight on his pelvis could hurt him.

"I'm scared." She stopped abruptly, pressing her forehead to his. "What if—"

"Then we try again." His words were soft and she combed his eyes for traces of pain.

"Help me."

Ellie pulled her hair over one shoulder. He fanned his hands over the flesh of her bottom, kneading gently, and lowered her onto his lap. The warmth of his hardness slipped between her lips in a delicate tease as he raised and lowered her against the smooth tip fueling her building ache for him.

"Ready?" she whispered.

Pat kissed her more desperately and Ellie reached behind her, guiding him inside and placing a touch more of her weight on him. Supporting herself with her back hand, she clenched the muscles of her pelvic floor around him, pressing upward again and again, to elongate the pulsing pleasure until her thoughts blurred and she splintered into a rush of sensation that jellified her limbs. Pat moaned in a mixture of exertion and determination and in an instant she was no longer supporting her own weight. His arms were around her, cupping her thighs from behind to control the pressure to his tolerance, moving her steadily faster. He thrust again, his face contorting into half-scowl and half-release as he kissed her softly, and moved her body over his length a final time. Ellie watched his eyelids flutter at the release, stroking his cheek and gently sliding to the side when he began to relax beneath her. The mix of relief and pride on his face told her there was truth in his joke about performance.

"I love you," she whispered, grateful again he hadn't been taken from her. A broken *this is us, healing,* floated into the darkness as she nestled into the crook of his arms and drifted into a troubled sleep.

Leila

"Time ain't exactly on my side, you know." Darla crossed her arms.

"I understand that. Thank you for taking a moment to reflect on my question." The counselor nodded and looked at Leila. "I asked your mother to spend some time in your shoes, and to ask herself what it is you think she could have done to better meet your needs as a child and as an adult."

"Wasn't hard to do." Darla pointed at Leila then looked back at him. "You listen to this one and I ain't ever done nothin' right. How about you ask her to walk in my shoes as a new mamma? She don't know what it's like to have a baby on your own."

"Can you tell us what it's like?"

"It's scary." Her eyes darted between the two of them. "You get pregnant even though you didn't mean to and you think, 'well at least I'll have this little someone who will love me no matter what.' Then the daddy gets with a new girl and your mamma is pissed because now she's got another bastard grandchild, but she takes you back in because you're blood. You keep your job as long as you can and pay her for the food you're eating, and then get fired right before your time because you're slow. A week later you're lying in a hospital bed, feeling like you been split open from one end to the other, but you look at this tiny little pink thing and just know you gonna take care of it no matter what—even though everyone thinks you're too young and too dumb. You gonna wrap your baby up and take her home."

"And how was it when you took her home?"

"It was good at first. Daddy couldn't stop telling Mamma how pretty Leigh Anne was. He even gave her a bottle once. I kept you wrapped up in a blanket my granny made for me when I was a baby and I would sit on the end of my bed and rock you for hours. They said you weren't supposed to sleep with babies in those days because of they might stop breathing, so I emptied out a drawer in my dresser and folded some sheets and towels in the bottom to make it soft."

She coughed and Leila couldn't help thinking that was what people did for newborn kittens, not infants. Sometimes, she forgot how young her mother had been when she was born.

"Then, I put a music box at the end." She stopped and gulped several deep breaths from her oxygen mask. "It had this little ballerina in a lavender ballet dress and pink tippy-toe shoes on top. You loved that music, Leigh Anne. It would stop your crying every time. Sounded like wind chimes, dah-dahdah-dah-duh-de-daaaah-dah," she mimicked the notes and a chill ran down Leila's neck as an ember of memory stirred in the recesses of her mind.

"Für Elise," she stared down at her hands. "That melody is called Für Elise. It's Beethoven."

"So you remember it?" The hope on Darla's face cut her like a razor.

"No," Leila managed to squeak out as an unnamed weight pulled at the back of her throat. "But maybe that's why I've always loved that piece of music."

"You said things were good at first." The counselor continued. "Did something change?"

"My brother and his girlfriend lost their apartment and moved back in to Mamma's with their kids. Those boys were loud and rough. Woke Leigh Anne up all the time and was always picking at her. I kept her in my room as much as possible. Just me and her."

She took another draw on her oxygen and stared wistfully into space.

"I used to love to dress you up. I would walk you over to the Goodwill every other day to see if they had anything new in pink. Then, I'd take them home and scrub them real good, even used the fancy washing powder I saved up to buy. I loved my baby girl, Mister. Wanted her to have the best of everything I could give her."

Darla put the mask back on her face and wiped a tear away with a yellowed nail.

"One day those boys, my nephews and Bobby's girlfriend's boy, they got to running through the house playing Army and one climbed up on my dresser. I was making a sandwich in the kitchen when I heard the crash. I ran back there fast as lightening, and you," she wiped her face again. "You were screaming. I couldn't get that damned piece of wood up off the ground fast enough."

Leila shook her head at the harrowing image of a helpless baby trapped as much by the dresser as by circumstance.

"Was she hurt?"

"No. Thank the Good Lord. She was scared senseless though and Bobby's girlfriend didn't do nothing to the boy. Said boys would be boys and I slapped her. Mamma said she was sick of us fighting and one of us had to go next time it happened. I was scared. I had my welfare, but nowhere else to go. I wanted a job, but I knew you would get hurt if I left you there without me."

Leila's universe shifted in the space of a second as she tried to wrap her mind around what Darla felt for her as a newborn and all she'd allowed to happen later.

"But you did leave, correct?" The counselor nudged.

"Yes. I got with Ronnie and he took us both in. That's why she calls him Daddy."

"I don't call him that," Leila shuddered.

"And that attitude is why you was always on his nerves! You ain't never been grateful for nothing he done for you."

Something inside Leila snapped and her braided hands shook with rage as every mark of Ronnie's belt on her flesh burned anew.

"I WAS A BABY!" she roared. "A baby! You got pregnant with Ronnie Jr. and that's why he quote unquote took us in! Don't pretend he was doing me any favors." Leila turned cherry red, mortified by her outburst, and sat up straighter. "You want to know the answer to his question? You want to know the one thing you could have done better? Not marry a man who was cruel to your child."

"He fed us! Clothed us! Worked nights and weekends to do that! If that ain't love, what else do you call it?"

"The minimum," Leila said, enunciating every syllable. "But I'll give him this; getting away from his hands and out of that house was one hell of a motivator."

Norah

"Thanks for meeting me."

"You're welcome," Norah answered, worried about the stress on Cami's face. "It sounds like we're both having less than stellar weeks."

"Isn't that the truth?" Cami smirked and passed her the wine list.

"I'm sticking with mineral water tonight, but you go ahead."

"Are you sure? Not strutting around that awful anniversary party seems deserving of a toast in my book. Walking out and calling him on his affair is deserving of two."

She cocked her head and Norah debated telling her about the pregnancy while she was still spotting. Cami turned the list over and picked up her phone.

"Kate says she's parking."

"Good. Tell me more about last night. How on Earth were you photographed with Marcus?"

"That's a long short story I'm afraid. I have been taking the overgrown children I work with to happy hours if they meet their deadlines and produce anything worth my time. He was at the bar and walked me to my car."

"So you didn't go together?"

"Of course not."

"Sorry," Norah rushed. "I'm just trying to catch up."

"It's fine." Cami checked her phone again. "I called Ellie to explain. She didn't answer so I left a message. I got a call from Jess an hour later asking me to meet with the firm's legal team. I'm not exactly sure how to read that one. Part of me hopes it's the time difference, but the bigger part knows she's angry and in defensive mode."

"Likely. She may also be trying to gather the facts via Jess. We all know Ellie is a planner first and foremost."

"I almost want to believe you," Cami laughed.

Kate's tall figure near the door caught Norah's eye. She had her cell phone to her ear and was standing with her back to the room. Norah watched her shift her weight from one foot to the other, thinking that even her fidgeting screamed of measured movements and extensive dance training. "Speaking of legal, have you heard from Mrs. Enrique?"

"No, but my lawyer thinks I should settle."

"Is that what you want to do?"

"No. Not yet."

Kate approached the table.

"But, it's getting harder and harder to remember that I didn't do anything wrong. That's not exactly my pattern lately."

"Hello!" Kate smiled and took a seat beside Cami. "Sorry I'm late. Cameron's therapist called as I was walking in."

"How is he?" Norah opened her menu to avoid Cami's eyes.

"Better," Kate said, looking only at Norah. "She thinks a visit from me and Liam would do him good. Zac was there today and convinced him to go for a walk. He, um, also called."

"Zac?"

"Yes. To talk about Cameron, and to ask if you were really dating the musclehead in the pictures."

"As if that's any of his business," Cami snapped. "What did you tell him?"

"That you weren't." Kate dropped her napkin in her lap.

"Was he who you—" Norah began and then swallowed the rest of her question at Cami's stony expression.

"Yes. He's the one I was talking about in the text." She rapped her knuckles on the table. "I told Kate, but no one else knows. It was beyond stupid."

"I'm not so sure about that." Kate's words trebled with her nerves and she took Cami's hand. "It didn't feel like he asked to be intrusive. I think he cares about you and is hoping he still has a chance."

"I know he does." Cami pulled her hand away. "But it was a one-time thing. I was a mess after the wedding and gave in to a monumentally selfish moment. It wasn't right and I knew it."

"That sounds familiar." Norah said, wishing her life had a rewind button.

"Sorry," Cami stammered. "That was insensitive. I only meant I knew it would mean more to him than it would to me."

Norah nodded her forgiveness, suddenly aware of the pungent smell of cumin in the air.

"But maybe it *is* right. He's always cared about you."

"Even if that's true, Kate, he deserves better. I pretended that night. I let myself slip away and imagine he was Blane and I hate myself for it. I woke up in Zac's arms and waited as long as I could to open my eyes and face what I'd done. Did you know he still wears Eternity, the same cologne they both loved in college? It was almost too easy to forget." She stopped and squared her shoulders. "He thinks he's in love with me and I used him."

Kate's eyes pleaded for support, but Norah had none to muster. She was the poster child for one night stands gone wrong. Having no idea what to say, she simply let the words "I'm sorry" leave her mouth.

"Thank you," Cami rapped her knuckles again. "New subject, please."

"I'm sorry, too," Kate finished. "I didn't mean to force anything on you."

"I know." Cami patted her hand and looked at Norah. "So, I'm updated on Mrs. Enrique. What about the bronze stallion himself? Any word from him?"

"Bronze stallion," Norah rolled her eyes, convinced Cami had a secret stash of trashy novels hidden away somewhere. "He texts or calls every day."

"And?"

"And I ignore them," she lied. Every time she didn't answer, she almost did.

Ellie

Ellie sat in Pat's sunny breakfast nook rereading the email from Jess and wondering if Cami was telling the truth or just going along with the spin. She knew Cami wouldn't betray her, but something about the way their arms were looped was too consensual to be completely staged.

"Good morning," Pat smiled and wheeled his way to the table.

"Good morning," Ellie repeated, worried he was in the chair instead of using his walker or cane. "More importantly, how are you? Are you stiff?"

"I'm fine," he laughed and kissed her forehead. "But I do love how you worry."

"Good Morning, Mr. Grayson!" The nurse's chipper voice echoed intrusively off of the walls. "I'll only be a moment with your tea."

"Thank you." He took Ellie's hand and put it to his lips. "I promise I'm fine. A little stiff, granted, but nothing more."

"Here you are, sir." The nurse bustled in and placed a tea tray in front of them. "I brought two mugs should Ms. Lindsay fancy something kinder to the digestion than her coffee." She winked expectantly at Ellie who still hadn't learned to like hot tea in the morning.

"That won't be needed, Emma."

""But thank you." Pat added.

"Very well. On to other business. Now that you're resuming your lovers' tangle," she grinned to let the cleverness of her euphemism register, "you'll find this on your tray for the remainder of the week. Dr. Havens wants it tested for bacteria so we can head off a UTI if need be. It's procedural."

"Of course." Pat cleared his throat and moved the plastic sample cup to the side of the tea tray.

"Enjoy your breakfast! I'll be about my duties now if you haven't any questions." She waited the requisite thirty seconds then flipped her stethoscope over her shoulder and padded out of the room.

"I'm grateful to need this." Pat nudged the edge of the cup with a coy grin and a slight tinge of pink to his cheeks.

Ellie smiled at the thought of the sheer relief in his eyes after he climaxed and the warmth of his skin on hers as their breathing steadied and they sank into the joy that was reclaiming the last bit of intimacy that had been stolen from them.

"Me too." Ellie took his hand, determined to enjoy the moment despite the incessant ding of incoming messages erupting from her phone.

"Is everything all right?" Pat stroked the top of her knuckles with his thumb and glanced at her screen.

"Yes." Ellie lied, skimming Jess' text and typing a reply.

Reply: To Jess Cell

Find out what Marcus wants.

"Why the frown, love?"

"Honestly? I was thinking about a picture I saw earlier."

"Was it us?"

"No. Thankfully, it has very little to do with you."

"How refreshing."

The lilt in his tone told her he wasn't convinced. She looked at the curve of his mouth, knowing she had every justification not to tell him about Cami and Marcus. This was her problem to interpret, not his. It was, quite possibly, the only one of her problems that didn't involve him, yet she felt compelled to tell him. More than that, she *wanted* to tell him.

"There's something else you need to know about someone who used to be close to me."

"You can tell me anything."

The sincerity on his face made her ignore the voice that told her to stop now and insisted that she could fix this before he *had* to know.

"It's Marcus."

Ellie tapped her foot as the name registered on his face and wished she had lied.

Leila

1 New Text: From Norah Cell

Missed you tonight.

1 New Text From Wes Cell (ICE)

No end in sight and this bid has to go out tonight. Please don't wait up. I'm sorry.

eila's calendar app lit up the screen with the color-coded notifications she had set.

1st day of daycare (Julia)
Send Show and Tell with Clara—Letter D
Department Meeting: 9:00
Syllabus Review with Dean Allen: 12:00
Medicaid Fee Structure with Hospice Liaison: 1:00 (Darla)
Muffins for bake sale
Visa payment due
Dance enrollment deadline

Proof Annabel Chen Blog
ID Badge Photo: 1:30
Annotations for first lecture due
Pick up birth control RX

Just another day in paradise, Leila thought sarcastically as she shifted Julia to her other hip and unplugged her phone from the charger.

"I love you, Mommy." Julia squished her cheeks between her rosy little hands.

"I love you, too, sweet girl." Leila kissed her forehead and stifled the welling anxiety that she would drop her at daycare for the very first time in the morning. "You're going to have so much fun at school tomorrow."

"So are you, Mommy!"

"Mommy! My toothpaste won't go on!" Clara called from her bathroom.

Leila walked down the hall picking up a trail of cast off clothing and toys that had somehow reappeared from their bins after clean up time. Her shadow looked back at her in the sheen of her hardwood floor, mopped by someone else, and she reminded herself that these were good problems to have.

Kate

Kate held Liam a little tighter as the nurse wiped the smear of chocolate pudding from the paralyzed portion of her brother's slackened face. She listened to Ken ramble on about MLB pitching trades and looked anywhere and everywhere except at Cameron's scar. Nevertheless, her mind's eye traced the perfect little white lines crimping the tri-colored pink flesh that remained of his right cheek. He had never intended to survive. That much had always been clear. Liam blew bubbles and clapped, happily oblivious to the tension in the room as Kate wiped the drool from his chin with his bib.

"See, we can do things together, buddy." Cameron choked out a morbid laugh and pointed to the chocolate covered rag in the nurse's hand. "Later, they can wheel us around while we crap our diapers."

Ken laughed and Kate cringed at the parallels between care for her infant son and for the older brother she'd both lost and not lost on that wretched day.

The afternoon she found him would be forever etched into her memory. She'd flown through the door, livid that her family's attorney had managed to strike Zac's honest testimony about the accident from the court record via a technicality. Cameron was set to testify the next day and she knew it was the last opportunity for him to tell the truth and confess that he, not Blane, had been driving the jet ski and that their family, not the Greenes, were responsible for the damages and injured property.

She remembered stomping upstairs and bursting into his room, yelling, "Look, Cameron! I get that you lied because Mom insisted and you were scared, but it's gone too far! Blane's family doesn't deserve this! It will bankrupt them on top of everything else they've lost! Cameron? Cameron! Where are you? Are you in there snorting coke? Isn't that what got you into this mess in the first place?"

She had thrown her weight against his bathroom door, expecting it to be locked, only to tumble headfirst into the smell of smoldering flesh. She would never forget the web of blood that covered the antique mirror and dripped down the walls in tiny red rivers as she crouched beside him on her mother's favorite embroidered towels- the ones that never left the guest suite- certain he had lined the floor with them intentionally.

Cami

"Why in the world are you here so early, Clark?" Dean Gatz' boisterous laugh filled the space as Cami rolled her eyes and spun her chair away from the editing bay to face him. He stood tall in the doorframe, wearing a white Under Armour shirt and navy blue basketball shorts.

"Why, hello, Kettle. My name is Pot."

"In my defense, I was headed to the gym, but my racquetball partner cancelled."

"My excuse is that I get more done without the interruptions," Cami answered, frowning as she recognized the blazing red letters of the *LA Talks!* logo on the rolled magazine in his hand.

"You play, by chance?"

"No. I mean I have once or twice, but it's been years. Do we need to, um, talk about that nonsense?" she asked, new anger at Marcus bristling the hairs on her neck.

"That's what I was going to ask you." He took a long stride toward the leather chair in front of her desk and sat with his elbows on his knees. "Look," he tore the glossy cover from the magazine and slid it across to her. "We both know the headlines in these rags are bullshit and completely dependent on what they had the chance to buy."

He waited for her to answer and she looked away into the stagnant silence, wishing she could un-see the photobox that read *PatSon's Frenemies: What They Don't Know CAN Hurt Them.*

"Tell me it's nothing, and I'll be on my way."

"I can tell you it wasn't what it looked like. Tell me your concerns for the company and I can give you a better answer."

"Ellison Lindsay's firm is not an enemy I want to make. Scratch that. Her firm is not an enemy I can afford to make."

"What are you implying?"

"The companies that pay us to develop the art for their ads will drop us in a New York minute if the magazines won't print them. The fastest way to die in this business is to alienate the mags. If Ellison Lindsay blacklists us because her 'frenemy' is my creative director, real publications—the ones that pay our bills—unlike this upscale trash," he thumped the magazine, "can't book Hollywood's finest if the story runs next to anything we've developed. Who do you think they're going to choose? Our work doesn't sell magazines; magazines sell our work. Trust me when I say no one messes with Ellison Lindsay."

"Again," Cami countered, "it's not what it looks like. Marcus tips off the paparazzi for attention. He *wants* to be a headline. Ellie knows I would never—"

"I'm not saying you would," Dean lowered his voice and stood at the sound of a computer booting up in the lobby. "I'm just giving you the courtesy of a heads-up that I won't have a choice if this escalates and the board sees it as a conflict between the company's rep and someone I just brought on."

"Understood," Cami turned the jagged page face down on her desk and spun back to the editing bay.

"But, if I did, I would choose you. You are hands-down the best I've ever seen." Dean left, closing her door behind him.

Ellie

"I'm not sure I understand," Pat said. "We are talking about the Marcus who found his clothes hurled out onto the street are we not?"

"Yes. The same."

"The very Marcus who stole money from you and sold private information about your clients to the press?"

"Yes."

"And now he's been photographed with your close friend?"

"Yes. I think he staged it to stay in the news. He has a lot to gain from being associated with me."

"As in he wants back into your life?"

Back into echoed in her ears as she realized Pat didn't know she had purposely kept Marcus on the fringes of her life as her trainer.

"As in he's a fame whore," she covered. "He will do whatever he can to grab a place on the *"PatSon"* coattails. Hurting me is simply a bonus."

The skepticism in Pat's eyes spurred the guilt sweeping through her.

"Let's not give it any more energy at the moment," Ellie said. "I want to enjoy my last few days in London with you and let Jess deal with his antics."

"Please don't give me the spin, Ellie. I can see that you're worried. First you say it has nothing to do with me, and then you say he wants to use us to extend his fifteen minutes of fame. There's more, isn't there? Be honest with me."

"You're right. There's something I haven't told you about an arrangement I made with Marcus years ago. It means virtually nothing, but looks terrible given the context and I'm worried about how he will use it."

Pat's brow creased and Ellie accepted that he would have every justification not to forgive her for what she was about to say. Part of her mind spun the fallout, and the other part spoke from her heart.

"Do you remember me telling you that I went to Cinque Terre after the relationship ended?"

"Of course I do." He pushed himself backward from the table like he was bracing to stand. "He betrayed your trust, broke your heart, and you left to recover. What else is there?"

Ellie blinked hard and put her hand on his knee. "When I came back, I had nothing. No job, no home, nothing but my sisterfriends and a handful of interviews. To add insult to injury, I hated that I missed him."

"So you went back to Marcus?"

"Not exactly. Please understand I could tell you a half truth right now instead of risking your reaction and I'm choosing not to."

Pat frowned.

"While I was in Italy, I blacklisted him as a thief and left his name as persona non grata at every upscale gym and fitness studio in town. I spread word of his affinity for selling secrets to his personal training clients and they dropped him one by one. By the time I came home, he had exhausted all of his prospects as well as what he had stolen from me. I waited a few months until I knew he couldn't find work and was couch surfing to approach him with an offer."

Pat stared at her with new eyes and she forced herself to finish.

"I met him at a coffee shop and handed him two envelopes. One was a bus ticket back to Pittsburgh, his hometown he hated. The other was a contract. I think—no I know—he is positioning himself to use it against me."

"What kind of contract?"

"The scorned woman kind that comes with an outlandish interest rate. It stipulated that I would call in favors to find him a position in an elite gym, allowing him to stay in LA, and he would repay every single cent he stole from me, lost earnings included, by acting as my personal trainer at the hours of my discretion, without pay, for a minimum of five years or until his debt was recouped." The color drained from Pat's face and she added, "No touching."

"So, ruining his mediocre career wasn't enough? You also made him some sort of indentured servant just to keep him in your life?" His eyes bored into her and he rubbed his temples like he was translating her words from a foreign language. "To control him? And you think that means 'virtually nothing?' Damned right you should worry about how he will use it! You can't OWN people, Ellie! For the love of God!"

Pat spun on his wheels and pushed himself to the doorway. He looked back at her only once before shoving the doors open and a lump tore at her throat.

1 New Text: From Jess Cell

I already have. He wants a job on one of our pro-athlete's campaigns and to be absolved of a prior contract with you. He insisted you would know what he meant.

I'd sooner hire Hannibal Lecter as my personal chef, Ellie thought walking through the double doors that were still swinging from the force of Pat's exit. He sat in front of the living room's bay window, staring down at the garden below, with his back to her. She put her hand on his shoulder and he tensed.

"I don't know what to say except that I am not the same person I was then, and I should never have forced him to stay in my life. It was childish."

"I'm not angry that you have an ex-lover who is still part of your life." Pat paused and tugged at the collar of his shirt. "Look at my history with Blythe. She's part of my inner circle now, but things were a bloody nightmare after the break-up and we literally didn't speak to each other for a full year until filming for the third *Destiny* film began." His voice trailed off and he turned to face her. "What I'm trying to say is that even as angry as I was then and how publicly humiliating her betrayal became, I never wanted her to suffer. I guess I'm just stunned you could be so, well, frankly..."

"Vengeful," she finished for him before he could settle on something more vicious.

"Yes. Can you put yourself into my position and imagine my alarm? What happens if you and I end badly? Am I in store for the same torture?" The raw hurt on his face deepened as he took her hand and pulled it to his chest. "This. What we have and what we've been through. All that we're trying to build. What did any of it mean if we could end like that? With you hating me, and me fearing you?"

"I would never," she said, pulling her hand away and resenting his implication that the two scenarios were in any way equal. Marcus had used her, to her ruin, for a meal ticket and a connection to the industry. He was still using her. He didn't have a voice in the press because he was on the fringes of her life; he had a voice in the press because Pat was now at the center. "Are you telling me you want to script our ending to protect yourself? Should I have our statements drawn up? Do you want me to sign an NDA?"

"No, Ellie. Of course not. I'm telling you why what you did to him struck a nerve. You're a powerful woman and I want to know you would never do anything like that to me."

"How can you not see that this is different?" She drew a sharp breath before he could answer. "I, I, don't have the words to list the millions of reasons why I would never do that to you, or to anyone ever again, but," her throat clenched and he touched her face. The relief in his eyes told her she was forgiven and she pressed her cheek into his hand, whispering, "Because that wasn't love. I could never do that to someone I loved.

I know that a thousand times over now." Ellie pulled away from him. "A thousand times over because of what we have right now."

"I apologize for storming out like that." He pushed a stray wave from his forehead. "Can you understand that I was as blindsided by this as you were the morning Scarlett's ridiculous engagement claims broke?"

"I definitely can." Ellie took a seat on the windowsill beside him. "And when you said it was a lie, and that the two of you were over, I trusted you."

"As I am you now." He ran his thumb under her jaw, tilting her chin up to face him. "Thank you for telling me the truth when you didn't have to. It means the world."

"I know." Ellie felt the balance restoring between them and resolved to remove Marcus from her life permanently—not for Pat, but for the person she wanted to be.

"I've just one final question." He broke into a wide grin and half-laughed, half-asked, "Is there anything else I need to know?"

"Not funny!" Ellie batted his hand away, caught off-guard by his humor, and slid into his lap to kiss and make up.

"Mr. Grayson?" The nurse's voice followed a soft knock.

"Lie to me and tell me we have a few more moments alone." Pat rolled his eyes and pressed his forehead to hers.

"We can dream." Ellie tapped the end of his nose and stood.

"Come in, Emma."

"Your mum is here, sir. Shall I tell her she's quite early and give you two another minute?"

"That won't be necessary, Emma. You can send her in."

"Don't you dare!" Ellie cinched her lilac kimono more tightly over her slip.

"Very well. Please tell her Ms. Lindsay isn't decent but her son is a pillar of chastity." Pat ducked his head and threw his hands up over his face to block an imaginary blow.

"You, sir, are intolerable." Emma chuckled and stepped backward through the doors to the kitchen. "I'll tell her you will be in shortly."

Pat turned his wheels, eyes bright as he inched toward Ellie and pulled her back into his arms.

"We're supposed to be getting dressed," Ellie said inches from his lips.

"You Americans. Always in such a hurry. It's tragic really."

"True." She stood and rolled her shoulders so that the silk fell to the floor. "Chop-Chop, now!"

Ellie sauntered over to the reverse tinted windowpane, pressing her back against the cool, deceptively clear, security glass.

"Maybe just a tease before intermission?"

Pat ducked his head, smiling broadly as he scooped up her robe and pushed himself toward her. A familiar tingle ran down her spine as she noticed again that his eyes never left hers in these moments.

"And an encore tonight." He nipped a line from her navel to her breastbone, pulling up her slip and walking his fingers down to the apex of her thighs, tracing first one smooth crease, then the other over her thong. He draped the soft robe up over her right shoulder, grazing a circle around her left breast with his thumb, and guided the fabric up over her other shoulder.

"I was promised a matinee," she quipped and he pulled back with a sudden pensiveness that dampened the energy between them.

"I'm going to miss you, Ellie. I keep forgetting how close it is."

"I know," Ellie leaned into him praying he wouldn't ask her to stay.

Norah

Half of her conflicted brain recounted every twinge in her uterus over the last forty-eight hours and touted medical probabilities. The other half desperately hoped she was carrying something positive from the present unknowns into her future. She waited ten minutes into the lunch hour, listening to the hallway grow still before making her way to the ultrasound suite. Jillan stood by the table and offered her a drape.

"Can we all agree to do away with formalities in this case, okay?" Norah asked, pulling her shoes off one at a time. She untied her scrubs and slipped them and her panty-liner-laden underwear to her ankles before lifting herself onto the table.

"Whatever happens," Jillan's calm voice broke her concentration as she positioned her feet in the stirrups and shimmied into position, "you *are* a mother now. Stay as clinical as you need to be to feel comfortable, but just remember that the love you felt for that little blip on the screen is different from anything else on God's green earth. We're going to know what's going on in a hot second, but that does not take away from what happened before. You lock that love up deep in your heart where it belongs. Okay?"

"Yes, friend," Norah replied in a soft whisper as she wiggled her toes in anticipation of the insertion. Her heart raced beyond her control as the screen went through the routine static and the wand scanned her uterus. Her internal clock told her it had been less than fifteen seconds, but she willed the screen to show her an answer.

"Breathe." Jillan said as the waves of the heartbeat began to crawl across the lower edge of the screen. Norah stared at the pulse, taking in the healthy reading and clenching her eyes at the magnitude of the relief washing over her.

Kate

"I can barely stand to visit him and relive it all. In a way, I'm just as self-destructive as Cameron," Kate said looking into Leila's tired eyes and chapped lips.

"I disagree. You are far from it. I don't mean to imply I walked in your shoes, or in his, through Blane's death or the trial, but you were there for Cami and advocated for the Greenes as much as you possibly could. He could have done the right thing and told the truth about who was driving like Zac did."

"He didn't see it that way." Kate cut the piece of chicken in front of her, but didn't take a bite. "All he saw was an end to the pain he had caused."

"You ladies okay out here?" Wes poked his head through the back-door holding the bottle of wine they'd been sharing. "The girls talked me into one more show and then we're headed to bed."

"I can come help." Leila stood and Kate smiled knowing Wes wouldn't let her.

"I got this. Enjoy your break. You both deserve it."

"Thank you. We appreciate it."

Kate watched her friend blush, enamored that the love between she and Wes was so palpable.

"I'm sorry. You were saying?"

"Umm, I was saying that Cameron didn't see it as selfish." She took half a sip of wine. "It's twisted, but he told me more than once, just before my parents called for the appeal, that everywhere he looked he was the problem. He felt that without him, our parents, Blane's family, Cami, and Zac would have one less stressor. I don't think he saw another way out. He also thought he deserved to die. The cocaine definitely didn't help."

"I can see how that would be a hard burden to bear. Seeing your loved ones hurt because of your choices cuts deep."

"It does," she said crossing her legs and moving half of the bite she'd cut to the side before slicing another. "One Thanksgiving, the first after he was released from the rehab's transition house," she speared the smallest square of chicken and laid her fork on top of her salad, "my mother chose a liquid lunch over the food on her plate and advised a pregnant cousin to stop at one child to avoid competition between siblings. 'Look at my offspring,' I remember her saying with her best cocktail smile, 'their newest rivalry is to see who can accrue the biggest bill from the psych. ward.' I can still see their smug stares ping-ponging from her, to Cameron, to me. I was mortified. Cameron blew his nose as loudly as he could on his sleeve and left the table, and I," Kate looked at her fork, but didn't pick it up, "I nodded along with my grandmother's loud explanation that my mother was being dramatic and that I was simply talking to a nutritionist who also happened to be a counselor about my *anemia*. My mother followed suit and asked the cater waiter to bring me more prime rib in the interest of my iron levels. I'll never forget choking it down like every bite was a spectator sport. For weeks, every breath I took reminded me of its sinewy flesh and the smell of horseradish. I hit a new low and spent that Christmas on a feeding tube."

She shuddered at the hazy memories of being strapped down and fed under sedation, as helpless to stop it as she was to help herself. Kate took the bite from her fork, chewing it slowly and with the practiced intention of recovery.

"It sounds like you were both crying out for help." Leila glanced inside toward the quiet kitchen. "And for the control over your bodies and circumstance that you deserved."

"Thank the Lord cycles can be broken and we are not our mothers."

Kate cut another bite, hoping Leila knew she was already giving her girls the home they deserved and wishing she were doing the same for Liam.

Cami

"I don't know what to say except that I am sorry it happened." Cami turned her chair away from the noise on the opposite side of her office wall. "And I'm sorry for what it looks like."

"I understand."

Ellie's voice echoed tersely over the line and Cami rubbed her temples, thinking they should have had this conversation twelve hours ago.

"I fired him the night of the photograph and cancelled my membership to the gym. There shouldn't be any further association."

Cami felt her words fall flat and searched the flurry of thoughts in her head for what really needed to be said. She knew it was all about trust with Ellie, but she had no idea how to say she hadn't done anything wrong without it sounding like she had.

Leila

1 New Text: From Cami Cell

Help me talk to Ellie? She was an iceberg on the phone and I don't know what to say to her except that I'm sorry. I know how the pic looks, and what the article says, but I have never seen Marcus in that way.

eila read the text and repositioned her Chi. She could do this. With a little practice, she would have work-ready hair before the girls woke up, and still be there for the people who needed her.

Reply: To Cami Cell

I think she's reacting to the familiarity in the pic. Maybe stress that he reminds you of your brothers and your interactions are more sibling banter than flirtatious? Maybe if she sees it that way she will understand? It's no news to Ellie that he will jump at any chance he can to be on camera. Know she loves you even if she's feeling vulnerable at the moment. Being away from the firm isn't easy on her.

1 New Text: -From Cami Cell

Thanks. Good points. How's your mom?

Leila released her straightish hair from the flat iron and took a breath. The counselor was right. She made time for the things that were important to her. If it were her mom or Tanya, would she have answered immediately? Or would she have let it go to voicemail until she had time to deal with it? Why did Cami, whose tactless honesty hurt her feelings regularly, take precedent? What did that say about her priorities? Was she seeking Cami's approval and wanting to be Ellie's advocate? Was it her peacemaking tendencies? She looked at the dark circles under her eyes in the mirror as her mother's ringtone broke the silence.

Fancy don't let me down.

"Hello?" Leila answered with a conscious smile in her voice, determined to set the conversation off on a positive note.

"It's me," her stepfather's voice barked, "and I got somethin' to say to you."

"I—"

"No, girl. You don't get to say a word."

She flinched at his tone and her left hand rose automatically to her right arm, tracing the familiar wide grid of his fingers.

"It's my turn now."

"I don't under—" Leila began, hating the tremble in her voice as she looked at her hand and tried to reconcile why she was still shrinking under the words of a man who hadn't had any real control over her since she was a teenager.

"You're done talkin.' You've said plenty and none of it was what your mamma needed to hear."

Leila swallowed hard as Ronnie spewed on.

"I always knew you'd turn out this way. You were an ungrateful little bitch from the first time I held you. More. More. More."

The all-governing voice of her childhood laid into her with its familiar bite and she stiffened for his next blow.

"That was always your song. You ain't like the rest of us. You ain't never loved nobody but yourself. You got the world and can't spare a damned dime for your mamma or Tanya."

Leila leaned against the countertop in front of her and ignored the memories of clasping the doorframe and swallowing her screams as his belt rained down on her back and thighs. Ronnie snapped something unintelligible at a young voice that sounded like Tanya's son and clicked a cigarette lighter to life. The sound unleashed a fire inside of her and she pictured her mother and Ellie as scared, determined young women in hospital rooms and what they would want the her they loved to say in this moment.

"You're right. I'm nothing like the rest of you."

Leila gripped the counter as Ronnie erupted in a flurry of expletives and made herself finish.

"Not anymore. But not because of where I live or what I didn't do. But because I see through you. I see the man who bullied my mother into believing she couldn't be more than trailer trash and enabled her addictions and inadequacies to keep her under his thumb. I'm nothing like the rest of you because I'm not trapped. Not anymore."

The sharp crash of the antiquated receiver hitting the base rang in her ears, echoed by the shrill pulse of the dial tone and the pounding of her own heart. She stared at the mirror in disbelief until her breathing settled.

"And never again," she added, closing her eyes in a prayer of thanks to God for putting angels of grace on her path.

Ellie

"You look lovely, dear." Pat's mother stood as Ellie walked down the stairs into the formal living room and took her thin outstretched arms by the fingertips.

"So do you." Ellie squeezed her milky white hands warmly and noticed she was wearing the same black shift dress and pearls she had worn in the family photo on Pat's mantle.

"Thank you. I know I should have bought a proper black gown by now, but I love this dress. I've worn it to Patrick's high school commencement, my parents' Golden Anniversary, his brother's wedding, my grandsons' christenings, and to every other family occasion when I've been bursting with pride." Mathilda's eyes moistened and she sat. "And today I saw it hanging in my closet and it struck me that it was what I would have worn to his funeral. Apologies." She stopped and took a wadded lace handkerchief from her clutch. "I've been a little emotional this morning since putting it on. I'm afraid it's freshened the whole ordeal and taken me back to that awful night. There is no other way to explain the abject torture that was imagining my Patrick alone in a hospital with only that horrid agent of his and some Hollywood interlopers to look out for him until I arrived. My heart still stops cold just thinking about it."

Ellie cocked her head thinking his agent had never once visited.

"Of course, I hadn't met you—*the* Ellison—yet and didn't know you were different from the lot of them. In fact, Patrick had told me he planned to end things with you the night before." She blotted her eyes and dabbed her nose. "He promised to let you go back to your life so you wouldn't be hurt by all of," she pointed her index finger at the security camera mounted in the corner, "this."

"I can't say he didn't try." Ellie stifled her urge to squirm at the memory by tilting her sandwiched kneecaps to the right and crossing her ankles.

"I'm sorry if it hurt to hear, that night or at this very moment, but I still firmly believe that he had, and has, no right to drag you or anyone else with any hope of normalcy into his spectacle."

"You must forgive my mother," Pat's cool voice interrupted from behind them. "Now you know where I get the rambling from."

Mathilda blanched before rising shakily to kiss her son's cheek. Pat put his hands on her shoulders and whispered something sternly into her gray hair. She looked up at him with a mixture of concern and acquiescence then sat, fingering the strand of pearls around her neck.

"Again, please forgive my emotions today. They seem to have a mind of their own. Patrick and I are both quite fond of you. My fretting heart simply doesn't want to see you or my son hurt."

"Thank you." Ellie stood and looped her hand around Pat's waist. "I feel the same way."

"The mother in me is hoping an afternoon in the West End will persuade you into staying here with us."

"I truly wish I could," Ellie said, finding Pat's hand. "London has definitely charmed me."

"That's lovely, dear." Mrs. Grayson's eyes darted around the room and settled on the walker against the wall.

"She'll be back, of course," Pat said.

Ellie steadied him as he wobbled slightly on his cane.

"But when? And for how long?"

"For as long as is needed," he answered and chill bumps pricked Ellie's arms as she realized the turn this conversation was taking.

THE ACT: VOLUME II, THE CIRCUS OF WOMEN

"What's on your mind, Mathilda? I know there's tension about my leaving, but something tells me this goes deeper."

"As I said before, I don't want to see my son hurt. I think you are wonderful. And, um, intimidating. And I acknowledge that you saved Patrick's reputation when Blythe was unfaithful, and when he was photographed with that married pop singer, what's-her-name, and that you are refusing to let this tragedy define him. You will always have my gratitude for that. But..." She twisted the lace in her hands.

"But, what, Mum? What could possibly matter to you more than that?

"It's fine, Pat." Ellie squeezed his hand.

"Again, you and your firm have my unending gratitude for keeping the best of Patrick prevalent in the public eye. You always will, but, I, I think he might be confused. I cannot fathom him committing to someone who would leave him now. He still needs you. Here. In London."

Ellie stared into her earnest brown eyes, knowing she was speaking from the heart and wanted nothing in return but her son's happiness.

"She has a firm to run, Mother. Not to mention a life on hold in Los Angeles."

"This is true," Ellie said, choosing her words carefully. "Mathilda, I understand how terrifying it is to know someone you love is alone and in pain. I was in your shoes too as it all unfolded after the shooting. In fact, I was so horrified that I couldn't let go of my friend Leila's hand on the tarmac and practically dragged her on the plane with me. I knew I could be his advocate, but I needed someone there who knew that I loved him and was terrified I might lose him. Leaving London has nothing to do with my commitment to Pat. I hope you will believe me when I say I have stayed as long as I possibly can, but that my firm, my livelihood, can't coast on alone indefinitely. I hope that you'll see this as me going back to LA to work for both of our futures and not as me abandoning him."

"She's not jumping ship, Mum," Pat said with a forced laugh. "Try and see that. For me."

"I will, but I worry about what's next for you." Mathilda lowered her head and pulled at her pearls.

"So do we," Ellie and Pat answered in unison.

Leila

"I love you, sweet girl." Tears pricked the back of Leila's eyes as Julia gave her a wet kiss and cheerily took her teacher's hand. "You're going to have so—"

"Much fun! I know, mommy! You can go to your work now."

"We'll take good care of her," Ms. Claudine, the head teacher, said gently.

"Thank you. I know you will."

"Class, let's ask our new friend Julia to come play!" Ms. Jessica, the assistant teacher, called from the rug.

"Bye, Mommy!"

Julia gave her legs a quick hug and ran toward the group without looking back.

"Are you okay?" Claudine asked.

"Yes," Leila's voice cracked. "I, I just didn't think it would be this hard. She's my youngest, and has never—"

"I promise to text you if she has anything less than a fantastic day. Just stop in at the desk and ask them to send me a note with your cell."

"Thank you. I appreciate that."

Leila let herself be ushered out of the brightly colored craft paper covering the classroom door. Ms. Claudine gave her a final wave and Leila stared through the window at her new normal.

1 New Text: From Tanya Cell

FYI Thanks a lot for making my day hell.
Mamma is crying bc of u. I have 12 hours to put in and have to leave her alone. Daddy is going to Junior's to help fix his car.

Kate

"Are you sure, babe?" Ken raised an eyebrow. "I can take the rest of the day off. The three of us could grab a bite to eat and hit the park."

"I'm sure. I just want to go home. These visits take it out of me."

"Okay, but promise me you'll rest during little man's nap."

"I will," Kate lied. She stood on her toes to brush her lips against his cheek. "Can you take him to the car while I sign us out?"

Liam reached for Ken with a high-pitched squeal and Kate kissed his rounded little fingers as they let go of her.

"I'll be right there," she said and turned toward the stone pathway that wound to the front desk. The smell of eucalyptus wafting from the lobby overpowered the smell of ammonia in the hallway, perpetuating the illusion that this was not a nursing home.

"I hope you had a nice visit, Mrs. Stone." The receptionist greeted her enthusiastically and tapped a cotton candy pink fingernail on the visitation clipboard.

"It was," Kate said, distracted by the woman's electric blue eyelids and the mound of white frizzy curls erupting from a magenta banana clip atop her head. She found Cameron's name in the log, then stopped short at what she saw. Cami's name filled the lines above Ken's messy cursive. Kate traced the dates and her stomach clenched. 9/11, 9/18, 9/25.

"Excuse me, but this 'Cami,' her visits are a new development, correct?"

"Mr. Prescott's friend? Oh, yes. She's been coming once a week with him. The nurses have caught on and started fighting for the Monday night shift. Just between us girls, your brother behaves better after they leave and Mr. Prescott ain't exactly bad to look at if you know what I mean? He also brings us these delicious little macaroons from his restaurant."

"Thank you."

Kate scribbled her name on the clipboard, hurt that Cami hadn't told her and wondering what, aside from Zac, had changed her mind after all of these years.

Cami

"This is the last time," Cami said, stepping into the warm air of Zac's apartment.

"Lies we tell ourselves."

He grinned and the scent of Blane's cologne warmed her cheeks.

"I'm serious this time. It's not right. It will never be right."

"You know I disagree."

"You deserve more." She pulled away from his reach, like she always did at first, and then let herself fall into the memories of the one she loved.

Norah

I New Text: From Matt Cell

I'm back from my parents' house. I stayed a few more
days. Not that you care. We need to talk about the baby. I
want an amnio, not a blood test. If it's not mine, I'm out.

orah rolled her eyes at his message. There was no way she was
having an amnio without medical cause.
"Are you okay?" Leila asked.
Norah silenced her phone, trying to remember what they had been
talking about.

"I'm sorry. That was Matt. He wants an amnio to prove paternity."

"Um, no. I can't believe he had the nerve to even suggest it. What
did you say?"

"Nothing yet. But it's a firm *hell no* without a reason bigger than his
ego. He's just going to have to settle for a blood test."

"Did he tell you about his fight with Wes? I don't think they've spoken since."

"No."

"Apparently, Wes wasn't as surprised as he expected him to be when he told him about Enrique and Matt got really angry. He said some rude things about me and told Wes he would never understand what it was like to have a wife who didn't put him first. Wes told him that was a two-way street and made a crack that happy wives have happy husbands. Matt called him a pompous ass and threw some money on the table before storming out of the restaurant."

"I don't even know who Matt is anymore, much less how we could possibly raise a child together civilly."

"Maybe that's what you make goal number one with the marriage counselor?" Leila suggested without a trace of her trademark optimism.

Ellie

"*For gooooood,*" the West End's newest Elpheba belted in a Tony-worthy treble and the veteran Glinda joined in perfect unison.

Ellie sat in awe of the powerful performance in front of her. She could not remember ever having been so transported by a musical before. Then again, she rarely went to the theatre unless one of her A-List clients was performing. Ellie thought of the times she had ducked into a dressing room for a quick 'break a leg' before curtain, or barely warmed her seat at the company box after intermission and hoped tonight was not indicative of what she must have missed. The duo's powerful portrayal of two souls who were never meant to connect so deeply, much less find their greater purpose from the other, rang too true for comfort. Falling for Pat had changed her life; almost losing him had changed her world. She would never be the same Ellie who sank into a deck chair night after night to watch the waves, oblivious to how lonely she was until he began to make her laugh.

"It's like they wrote this song about us," he murmured in her ear and brushed the back of her hand with his thumb.

"Changed for the better and changed for good," Ellie whispered, wishing there were a way she could stay without compromising her firm.

"Ask her not to go," Mathilda's quiet words were for her son's ears, but cannonballed into Ellie's conscience.

Leila

"Hi, Beautiful." Wes walked into the kitchen loosening his tie. "It smells great in here."

"Thanks," she said over her shoulder and returned to the mixing bowl she was scrubbing. "How was your day?"

"Long. Not great and not bad." He wrapped his arms around her waist and gave her shoulder a quick kiss, eyeing the oven. "Are you making brownies?"

"Butterscotch blondies, actually. I wanted to do something special for Pat and Ellie's homecoming so I asked his mom to send me the recipe for his favorite dessert. They freeze well and I am somewhat caught up on my classes."

"I'm surprised the girls didn't wake up. Those two are like bomb-sniffing dogs when it comes to dessert."

"Oh, they woke up. I may or may not have promised they could have one for breakfast and take one for their teachers if they went back to bed and stayed there."

"Sounds like day care's problem to me." He laughed and tossed his jacket toward the chair their girls had stood in to 'help' stir the gelatinous pea-based pasta they knew as Mac 'n' Cheese. God help Leila the first time her girls had the real deal in all its neon orange glory. Wes rooted around in the pantry and emerged with a box of one of the sugary 'secret cereals' he loved that she kept stocked out of view.

"I like that idea. There are leftovers from Sunday dinner in the fridge and I brought Norah's entire flatbread home from lunch."

"Leila don't waste food," he said in an off-key impersonation of Joey Tribiani.

Whereas Leila had adored *Friends* and could hold entire conversations using only allusions to the series like a second language, Wes had had no interest in it when it was popular. He had tried hard to love the final season when they were dating and had eventually picked up some of the more iconic phrases years later as she subjected him to reruns. In her mind, his effort to quote it was equivalent to his patience with her failed attempts to locate north, west, south, and east in the real world.

"Was she excited about your first day? Did you celebrate?"

"We didn't exactly get to that." Leila loaded the last Sippy cup into the dishwasher.

"Really?"

"She has a lot on her plate. Matt wants an amnio. He won't settle for a blood test."

"That's an asshole thing to do. Especially when your wife is an OB. I can't say it surprises me though. He's just not the Matt we knew anymore."

"I agree. I feel terrible for Norah. I'm glad she wants the marriage counseling, but I think she sees it as a quick fix instead of as a starting point. It's like she's trying to triage the wounds the affairs and Matt's resentment have caused so she can get to the next problem of how to deal with the baby."

"I can see that. I spend my days fighting fires in order of degree and time sensitivity. I am constantly reprimanding the project managers under me to be proactive and to squelch problems before they start. By the time their messes get to me, they are usually in deep shit only I can fix. And it's constant."

"There are definitely parallels between your worlds." She yawned. "And I'm not saying I don't see the logic in her triage approach. I'm saying I think her perspective is off. Marriage is hard. Parenting is harder and neither of those things can be done theoretically."

"That's true. I was a great dad before I had kids."

"You're still a great dad, Wes. That's why we all want you here more."

"Believe me, I want that too. I'll start sending out my resume if that's what it takes."

$\mathcal{K}ate$

$\mathcal{K}$ate turned her face toward the soft light of the bedside lamp, loving the way the textured filaments of the pagoda-inspired shade complimented the 1960s base she had distressed in brushed bronze. She toggled the original gold-plated switch to 'off' and closed her drowsy eyes to the white noise of the baby monitor and the sound of running water as Ken showered after his evening jog. Thoughts of her favorite beach drifted through her mind, trailed by images of shimmering sand and whitecaps stretching up to meet the pale orange of the setting sun. Kate melted into the pure warmth of encroaching darkness and the distant promise of refreshment.

A whisper she knew tickled her ear once, then twice, and she burrowed deeper into her cocoon. The tickle of something wet on her neck made her flinch. Another toothpaste scented intrusion pierced the darkness as she strained to stay in the nothing.

"Mmmmm...you smell so good."

Ken's voice echoed, chasing the mistress that was deep sleep further into the blackness. She turned her body away from it, desperate to chase the peace as he nuzzled her neck and did everything that no longer turned her on. It had been three weeks. She should.

"Okay." Kate opened her eyes to slits with the enthusiasm of a sedated sloth. "We can have sex."

"Are you sure?" Ken asked, already pushing the sheet toward her ankles.

"Uh-huh." She hoped the obligation in her consent would register and he would let her drift away again, but he was halfway to her breasts before the last syllable left her lips.

"Does that feel good? I just shaved."

"Uh-huh." She craned her neck to see the clock over his shoulder. Liam would wake and nurse at 11:00, two hours from now.

"Just tell me what feels best. I want it to be good for you."

"That's sweet, but can we just cut to the main event? I am exhausted."

Kate looked up at the disappointment on the face of the man she loved and wished she wanted him. She *really* wished she did. More than that, she wished he hadn't woken her up.

"Okay. Only if you're sure."

He leaned over to the nightstand and pressed a button on his phone, filling the room with Marvin Gaye.

"It's fine."

Kate pulled her camisole over her head and tugged her underwear off. He put his arms on either side of her and she turned her neck away from his lips. He found his position and Kate felt the wobbly flesh of her stomach ripple into flabby waves with his entry.

"You feel amazing."

Kenny Loggins' voice replaced Marvin Gaye's and beckoned them to Pooh Corner.

"Damn. The playlist ended," Ken frowned but didn't reach to change it.

Drops of warm milk trickled from her breasts and pooled into cool wet circles under her shoulder blades as Ken finished to the tune of *Baby Mine*. Kate counted the precious minutes of rest remaining and considered cancelling on what was sure to be a late night at Ellie's tomorrow.

Cami

"But I am on the cleared list."

"Yes, you are. That's why you don't require an escort. We are scanning every license that enters the community and holding any going to Ms. Lindsay's property until exit. Non-cleared persons will be escorted to and from by one of us. We apologize for any inconvenience to your evening."

Cami left her driver's license begrudgingly with the security guard, resenting Ellie's overkill. Did she really think she could protect herself from another break-in by demanding extra duties from the glorified mall cops in the guard shack?

"So, I can pick it up from you in an hour? When does your shift end?"

"Yes ma'am. I will be here all night."

"Thanks," Cami said more to the parting rod iron gates she had driven through a thousand times than to the guard and regretted letting Leila and Kate talk her into this. Ellie paid good money for grocery delivery. There was no feasible way she had forgotten to have her refrigerator re-stocked after so much time away.

1 New Text: To Leila Cell

I had to leave my ID with the guard. Does Ellie even want
us here?

Cami voice texted the words, certain nothing could ever be the same
regardless of how many 'touches of home' they fabricated for Ellie.

Leila

The chilled, stagnant space looked like Ellie's living room, but it didn't feel like Ellie had ever been there. In many ways, that was true. Kate had outdone herself restoring the slashed sofas, shattered décor, and ransacked rooms back to the originals, but they both agreed Ellie needed more than a replication to feel like she was truly coming home. She and Kate hoped tonight's final touches would be a balm to at least one wound the vandals who called themselves Christians had left in their wake. Leila slipped off her flats and walked out onto the deck. All traces of the spray paint, animal entrails, feces, and broken glass were gone. She left the door cracked to bring some of the sea breeze scented peace Ellie loved into the living room.

A rapping 1-2-3 knock on the door told her Cami was here and she prayed Norah and Kate weren't far behind. She would never be able to justify this evening to Cami on her own.

"Cami! I'm so glad you could come!" Leila said, immediately registering the annoyance on Cami's face and forbidding herself from chattering about why this was time well spent for their friend.

"You're welcome. I still can't say I see the point. Where do you want me to start?"

"Would you mind taking some measurements? Ken said he would make some removable ramps for the deck stairs if he knows the width of the entryways. Pat is mostly using his cane now, but still needs the wheelchair after too much exertion. The measuring tape is by the cooler on the counter."

"Like Ken has time for that," Cami scoffed, looking at her phone. "Crap. Kate is lost and texting me. She's been here a zillion times. Why would she go north on the freeway?"

Cami's chunky heels made tracks in the freshly shampooed carpet as she crossed the room to the patio. Leila took a deep breath and tried to imagine how hard it must be for her to prep a homecoming for someone's love who had survived the unthinkable after burying hers.

"I'm here! I know I'm late, but a surgery sprang up," Norah's voice crackled through the intercom.

Leila rushed back to open the front door. "No worries!" She took Norah's bag and whispered, "I am so glad you came. Help me with Cami? I couldn't *not* tell her we were doing this, but I also knew how tough it would be on her. She's clearly stressed and I have no idea how to make it easier."

"I know."

Their eyes locked on Cami pacing around the deck and waving her hands like an air-traffic controller as she tried to direct Kate to Malibu.

"Can you imagine? Seeing all of this and wondering what if?"

"My thoughts exactly. It's so easy to see the could-have-beens when the pain is your present, instead of the 'ares' and 'could-bes' hovering in the future."

"Isn't that the cold truth? I'm starting to believe our entire lives are all one bad turn short of the 'what ifs' and 'what-could-have-beens.' Lord knows I am living it as we speak."

"Do you think you'll tell them about the baby tonight?"

"No. Not like this."

"How are you feeling?"

"Exhausted." Norah answered bluntly and Leila thought better of commiserating.

Ellie

A deafening crash split the air as they made their way down the steps of the theatre in the West End. Ellie's feet fell out from underneath her and she plummeted thousands of feet toward the sharp black asphalt. Her thoughts swam in a garble of screams and she twisted her forearms into a pretzel to break her fall.

"Ellie! Ellie! Wake up, love!"

Ellie bolted upright in a cold sweat, her heart racing around Pat's steady "Shhhhh...I've got you. You're safe." His silhouette grew clearer in the darkness and he folded her into his arms, whispering a soothing "there now" into her hair.

"I'm sorry, Pat. I, I, it was so..."

"Real." His body stiffened beneath her. "Believe me when I say I understand."

The stark reality of his night terrors had chiseled its own space in their bed even though Pat went to great lengths to hide them. In their first nights out of the hospital, under the sleep meds, his nightmares had been so intense that he had woken in convulsions and she'd had to wake the nurse for an extra dose of Vicodin to ease the aftermath. Try as she might, she would never reconcile the terror in his eyes as he re-lived what those monsters had done as a simple trick of the psyche. Each time his sleep talk escalated into panic, she would wake and run her hand through his hair hoping she had caught him early enough to be the bridge that diverted restless sleep from full-on terror. Oftentimes, he called for Blythe, but woke to Ellie. Far too frequently, she would wake hot (thanks in large part to what passed as air conditioning in Britain) and see him staring at the ceiling. She would ask if he wanted to talk about the dream, or was in pain, and he would say, simply and in monotone, that he was 'just processing the lot.' Ellie had no way to know if this was healthy or derivative and his PTSD counselor wouldn't return her calls.

What she did know was that she should have been there on the carpet. She never would have let him turn around for anyone not planted or rush-screened. Every new night terror gave her a front row seat to the hell he had endured that she could have easily prevented by sending a PA or a rep to fetch the girl with the shaved head.

"It's times like these that make me regret it all, Ellie."

"Including me?"

"Yes and no. I'm furious about the pain I've caused you. We should be scheming our first holiday away together, not prepping for a bloody trial and waking in screams because some entitled bugger played God. I want to go back to when we were still dreaming about us. Worse than that, I don't want you to leave even though we both know you must."

"I can't stay, Pat."

"I know."

He closed his eyes and Ellie stared at the ceiling in silence.

Norah

"These are addictive, Leila. How did you know they were his favorite?" Norah asked as she popped the last bit of blondie into her mouth.

"I asked his mom in the hospital. We had a lot of time to chat in the waiting room, and I knew I wanted to do something to make the homecoming easier on all of them. She sent me the recipe and even shipped the candied hazelnuts she uses.

"Sounds like a mamma's boy if you ask me." Cami resealed the container of brownies and popped it into Ellie's freezer.

"I think it's sweet that he's close to his mom," Leila added warily.

"There are definitely worse qualities in a man," Kate said, giving Cami a warning look and examining the various types of quinoa salads Leila had packed in mason jars. "I can't believe you did all of this. It must have taken you ages."

"Thanks. I just really wanted her to come home to something besides work and an empty condo. The hardest part was finding that balsamic vinegar she uses on everything. Did you know it's imported? She orders it by the case from Cinque Terre."

"Why didn't you just ask the housekeeper? Surely she would have sent you a picture of the bottle."

"Maria quit after the break-in, Cami. The Holy Pearls hate Catholics too. They call them false idol worshippers and detractors from the Church. Maria's husband and sons were worried about a repeat attack and begged her to find a new position. Ellie understood, but took it hard after trusting her for so many years. She had already fired her grocery service, pool company, and anyone else who had access when the break in and vandalism happened. That's why I wanted to do this. She's coming home to nothing familiar but work, and there are new normals there as well."

"So, her balsamic is from Cinque Terre?" said Norah. At last, something healthy sounded appetizing and she made a note to get a bottle.

"Yup. Bottled for eleven generations by the family who owns the hotel she always stays in. You should try one of those dairy milk candies beside the Twinings tin. The story behind why they're Pat's guilty pleasure is really cute. You see, even though they are a British staple, he hated them as a child and only grew fond of them because the American *Destiny* director stress-ate them by the pound and would only talk scenes with Pat if he accepted one when offered. Mathilda and I had a good chuckle over that one."

"Mathilda?"

"Pat's mom."

"Of course you did!" Norah laughed, completely unsurprised that Leila had struck and kept a connection with the woman. Leila had a knack for honing in on your best traits and showing them to you like a mirror. It was one of the qualities she liked best in her friend, and also the quality that leant her to being used so easily.

"What's she like?" Cami asked. "It's hard to imagine Ellie playing second fiddle to another woman in his life."

"She's sweet and very proper. She absolutely loves her sons to bits, but not in a my-boy-can-do-no-wrong mentality." She rushed the last few words and Norah knew she was referencing Matt's mom. "More like, I may disagree with his choices, but I love him anyway. She wants Pat to move back to London and still hopes he'll get a degree in science one day. She really did not want him to be an actor and despises the *Destiny* films. She loves *Life of Us* though. She said she wished he had started with a film like it versus chasing fame in such a, and I quote, *"commercial trainwreck of a character as Lucas Lucien."*

"I agree with her there," Cami laughed and poured puréed kale into the ice cube tray. "This smells like lawn in a bowl. You better add more blueberries to those smoothie packs, Kate."

"And it tastes just like it smells, but Ellie loves it." Kate scrunched her nose and scooped more berries into the freezer bags on the island.

"So, she and Ellie got along?" Norah asked, scanning Leila's checklist to see what more they had to do.

"That's hard to say. Ellie was in crisis management mode for most of their time together. She was on her phone juggling everything from the PR frenzy to having her locks changed and researching cryotherapy centers while we were in the waiting room, and then she was alone with Pat after the surgeries. Did I tell you I tripped and spilled water on him? I was—"

"Like I said, it's hard to picture Ellie playing second fiddle to another woman. Even if she is Mr. Hollywood's mom." Cami tossed the Vitamix into the sink and filled it with water.

"It sounds like she's very nurturing." Norah smiled at Leila. "It's no wonder you two got along so well."

"Thank you. I tried to be a comfort to them both, but it was hard. Ellie was cool and collected in front of Mathilda and the nurses, then darker than I've ever seen her when we were alone. She loves him and she loves the life she's built and she's terrified she'll lose one or both or everything. That's why I wanted us to do what the contractors and crime scene crews couldn't. Those brutes left nothing she loved untouched and I want us to give whatever we can back to her."

The butter laced essence of the brownie etched into Norah's throat and she took a chug of the ginger water Leila had brought for her.

Leila

"I still don't know what Ellie is thinking. I understand going to New York in the heat of the moment and being there for him post-op. I can even understand why she went to the rehab center with him. But London? She has all but moved to England for a treatment that is, at best, experimental. They were together all of what, three days before the shooting? There's no way she's in love with him enough to justify all of this. It's got to be guilt," Cami said, eyes closed, lying on the chaise lounge next to Kate, and ruining the sounds of the ocean with her pessimism.

"You're so hypocritical!" Kate giggled and threw an arm around Cami's shoulder. "You can't say you wouldn't have done the same thing if it were Blane. It would have been you, me, Zac, and Carolyn figuring out the next step even if it were spinal acupuncture in Katmandu!"

"Don't!" Cami snapped. "It's not even remotely the same."

Leila willed Kate to stop talking. She didn't have the energy to mediate a sobbing Kate after an argument with Cami, and Norah was already one foot out the door.

"I'm serious, Cami! You are being way too hard on Ellie. She's not stupid; she's committed. I think it's nice to see her open up after all this time."

"I'm on Cami's side here. It's a big investment so early in a relation-ship." Norah shrugged. "I'm all for Ellie taking a chance on happy, but I don't want to see her be a martyr either. She's not just tied to him now, but to his recovery as well. She's already given up too much."

"It's not like they're racing to the altar," Leila said, texting Wes that she was leaving in five minutes. "Besides, none of us have really seen them together. I've had a small glimpse and it was, I don't know, some-thing special."

"Coming from the person who thinks *everything* is special," Cami scoffed.

Anger welled up inside of Leila like waves breaking against a levy.

1 New Text: From Wes Cell

Awesome. Did you use the eye roll and scroll rule you use on Facebook with Cami?

1 New Text: To Wes Cell

So many times. Anyway, she gets a pass given the circum-stances. Don't wait up. I have to record a lecture when I get home.

Kate

"On that note, I think I'm heading home. I still have a lecture to record."

Leila looked like she was trying to hide her annoyance at Cami and Kate knew she was probably fuming inside.

"I'll follow you out," Norah yawned.

"You know you can stay always stay with me instead of funding the Hilton's third quarter. Unless you're not sleeping alone that is." Cami laughed and Norah shook her head.

"You're certainly in a mood tonight. But, thanks. I appreciate it."

"So, are you? Sleeping alone?" Leila asked, looking hopeful.

"Tonight, yes. Matt and I are at a crossroads and I have no idea what I want. Enrique is Enrique. He's over his marriage and ready to jump into a brand new future with me and I'm not. I want to give my own marriage a chance to work even though hemorrhoids rank higher on the list of the things I like than Matt does these days."

"You just compared your husband to a hemorrhoid and you're not sure if it's over?"

"It's more complicated than that, Cami. It's not just about me."

"For God's sake don't say you're pregnant."

Norah raised her eyebrows at Cami and Kate's heart didn't know whether to leap or sink.

Cami

Cami's jaw dropped and she tried to untwist her face from the involuntary 'you're-a-dumbass' expression that always got her into trouble. The absence of an excited shriek from Leila told her it wasn't news to her and she wondered if Kate had known too. They were always keeping things like this from her, as if she couldn't stand to watch anyone's life move forward.

"Seriously?"

"Yes, almost 12 weeks."

"Is it Matt's? Or?"

"There was an overlap. I know how Maurie Povich it all sounds, but I'm trying to focus only on the facts. I'm pregnant. I have strong feelings for someone who is not my husband and I'm not ready to close the door on either relationship despite the fact that Enrique and I make more sense together than Matt and I ever did."

The words resonated inside Cami like a bass drum and she knew now more than ever that she would never love Zac even if she wanted to. She could time travel with him indefinitely, but she would never love him.

"Maybe it's not about what makes sense." Cami gritted her teeth and tried to piece together the right words to say the impossible. "So what if you and Enrique mesh on paper? If you're holding back, there's probably a good reason. And I don't mean that you should stay with Matt just because you're not ready to go full steam ahead with the bronze stallion. I mean that you should trust your instincts."

"I agree with Cami," Leila said with her eyes on Norah.

"Not that I'm the expert." Cami looked at Kate and then back inside at the restored picture of Ellie and her sister hanging behind the white sofa. "While we're making announcements, you might as well know that I am still sleeping with Zac. It was an emotional Band-Aid after Gracie's wedding and I told myself I would never do it again. Then I did do it again, four times. I don't love him. I'll never love him. I'm just lonely and when I close my eyes he feels like Blane. He smells like him, thinks like him, and loves me like he did. Being with him is all I want to do all of the time for all of the wrong reasons. It's sick and it has to stop."

"So the better question might be are *you* sleeping alone tonight?" Kate asked and Cami simply shook her head 'no'.

Leila

eila wiped Clara's tears with the shoulder of her t-shirt. "Remind me how tall they are and what color of fur they have while I tuck you in?"

"Ten feet. They are ten feet tall purple bunny rabbits with tails made of rainbow glitter that shakes off in poufy clouds when they hop. That's what I'm going to pick to think about when I wake up scared."

"And if it doesn't work, you'll come to Mommy's bed. Right?"

"Ri-igh-ght."

Clara yawned and Leila straightened the sheets around her, hoping this would be the last nightmare and that she could log a few hours of sleep before Wes's alarm went off. She walked back through the house, turning off lights as she went, and sat down at her computer to finish recording her lecture about the labyrinth of gilded cages that was Gatsby's world for her Humanities through the Classics course.

Ellie

"**W**e'll never get you to Oxford now!" Mathilda exclaimed. "Can you believe it? Three nominations!" Ellie drummed her foot and turned the volume up on the live feed streaming from her computer.

"I truly can't."

Pat's eyes raced around the empty room and Ellie put her hands on either side of his face. She kept her eyes locked on his even though her mind was already spinning the statements they would make when the media inevitably called it a sympathy nomination.

"Three! This is going to be huge for you." She brought his lips to her forehead.

"It's bloody fantastic, I just can't beli—Roland's husband! I have to ring him. What time is it in the States?"

"Yes, go ring Mark. It's early, but he's likely up and listening."

"Four!" Ellie exclaimed as Tom Hanks listed the Best Actor nominees. "Four Golden Globe nominations!"

The last thing she saw before Pat's mouth found hers was Mathilda crack a sly smile through flushed cheeks at her son's public display of affection.

"Go!" Ellie pushed him away. "Go call Mark!"

"Four!" He kissed her forehead, counting "one," then each eyelid, "two, three," and planted a final peck on her cheek "four!" before bursting into laughter and shuffling out of the room on his cane.

"Don't overdo it, Patrick." Mathilda called after him.

"You must be so proud."

"I am. I haven't seen him happy like this since before the press and that other *Destiny* boy derailed everything he and Blythe had. He loves you. I'll admit at first I didn't quite see it, but I do now. You balance each other in a way they never quite did."

"Thank you," Ellie said, taken back by her sudden vote of faith and noticing again where Pat got his tendency for 'no filter' declarations.

"Which is exactly why I will shamelessly beg you not to leave now." Mathilda straightened nervously in her seat. "What will happen to him on the heels of this news? The microphones will surround our homes screaming that he doesn't deserve the nomination. They will find one hundred ways to say that it is a pity prize because a lunatic tried to murder him. What happens when he stops sleeping and starts reading The Holy Pearls' website again? Only now he's alone? What then?"

"Then, we deal with it. One stumble at a time. Therapy, PT, and faith will see us through."

Mathilda pulled at her scarf and Ellie softened, reminding herself they were on the same side.

"He's not a child."

"He's my child," Mathilda said with a tremble that squelched any joy that remained in the room from the nominations. "And I can't be there for him in the wee hours like you can."

"I know. I can't imagine how hard this is for you. He'll manage until he leaves for LA and then we'll be together."

"In America, Ellison? Where no amount of blood spilled changes the laws and where who knows who is still after him disguising vigilantism as the Lord's work? I may as well tell you now that I have asked him to move back to London permanently. His father, his brother's family, and I want him home. He belongs here. And," her voice broke, "if you truly belong together, you'll want what's best for him too."

She twisted the ends of her scarf impossibly tighter and Ellie curled her toes to avoid reminding Mathilda she was way out of her league when it came to confrontation.

"But my life is in LA and so is much of his."

"It doesn't have to be. He's been offered the part of Mr. Darcy in a modern-day adaptation of *Pride and Prejudice* in the West End. He loves the stage and it will keep him here and safe for a three-year engagement."

"How do you possibly know all of this?"

"Because Blythe will play Elizabeth. She's taken the role on the condition that he be offered Darcy. It's his to refuse."

"Yes, it's *mine* to refuse, Mum. You were wrong to tell Ellie before I had the chance." Pat's eyes burned with squelched anger. "I'm so sorry Ellie. You weren't meant to find out this way. It all came about this morning. My agent doesn't even know it's been offered."

"So you're considering it?"

"Yes." He ran his hand through his hair and glared down at his cane. "Again, Ellie, I wanted to tell you differently and after the trial. It's that I'm not sure LA is ever going to be the place for me again. At least not right now. I don't even know if I want the part, but I do know that I'm scared of being targeted again."

"I think I'll take my leave, Patrick."

"I think that's best," he said tersely.

Mathilda flinched. "I know you're cross, but show me out?"

"Excuse us, Ellie."

"Ellison, I'm sorry. I just thought you should know in case you want to consider opening a London branch of your firm." Mathilda huffed, "So he could be safe; so you both could be. So my future grandchildren could be. It's an excellent salary and a show to be proud of, Ellison."

"So *Life of Us* isn't something to be proud of, Mum? Don't delude yourself about the salary they're offering. It's a ten pence compared to what they're throwing at me to reprise Lucas in the *Destiny* prequel!"

"That may be true, Patrick, but think about the costs to stepping backward into a role meant for a teenager. You've lived that life. Your family wants you home. If you must act, do it here! Play Darcy. Get married. Start a family before your father and I are cold in our graves."

The worry in Mathilda's voice escalated to anger as she shouted at her son.

"Stop meddling in my life, Mum! I know you orchestrated this with Blythe. I may be crippled, but I am not stupid." Pat matched her volume, challenging her to deny the accusation.

"I was advised not to have children," Ellie blurted over their argument, "based on genetic markers for the pediatric cancer that killed my sister. Aside from that, I don't want to be a mother. There. Now we all know it all. I'm sorry, Pat. You weren't meant to find out this way."

She threw his words back at him and turned on her heel toward the stairs.

Norah

"Look, if you were done before we even sat down, tell me why we're here? Is this just another audience for you to lambast me in front of?" Norah crossed her legs angrily.

"Do you think I'm here for the coffee? We're here because you had an affair."

"And so did you."

"Let's get back to our goals," Dr. Crinson broke in. "Norah wants to rebuild respect. Matt, you want to be able to trust Norah. I want you to text something to each other once a day that reminds you of why you fell in love." The therapist pointed to the intentions they had just written.

"Fine, but I don't know how you ever get trust back with some mushy text messages after you lose it to this degree. I want to know if I'm going to be a father before I decide if I still want to be her husband."

"And that is not a condition for you. Correct, Norah?"

"Absolutely not. I won't subject a healthy pregnancy to an amnio. It's unethical and just another one of Matt's ego tantrums. I would consider something noninvas—"

"But she wants *me* to get tested for STDs."

"Pregnancy and venereal disease are two separate animals, Matt. Me wanting you tested is completely reasonable. You should do it for yourself if not for the baby or for me. Enrique and I used protection every single time. It was a nonnegotiable for both of us. I've been tested just like any other prenatal patient would be."

"Wait. I want to change my answer. We're here because Norah had an entire relationship with someone else. I don't think I care as much about the sex as I care about the room. They rented a room like they were playing fucking house. Which is apparently all we were ever doing, given that I was the only one pushing our lives forward. Half of the time, I thought she wasn't pregnant because she was still secretly on the pill and didn't want to be."

"That's ridiculous Matt."

"Is it, Norah? Who wanted to buy a house? Me. Who wanted you to cut back so we could actually be together on nights and weekends? Me. Who wanted a baby three years ago? Me again."

"And who kept charging up credit cards all the while telling me to cut back and slash half of our income? Office visits and a day surgery or two a month do not pay those bills, Matt. Much less our college loans or childcare for an infant!"

"Maybe that's why you're here," Dr. Crinson interjected. "It sounds like you're here to learn to communicate and to listen to one another. Matt, it sounds like you aren't certain Norah sees you as an equal or trusts you as a provider. Norah, it sounds like you think Matt's expectations are unrealistic and that he resents your success despite what it provides for your family."

"That's a start." Matt pulled his phone from his suit.

"Then that's where we begin." Dr. Crinson typed a note on her tablet and repeated her assignment. Norah knew then that she would only do it if Matt did.

Kate

K ate slowed her pace behind the stroller as they neared the final curve before the hill, lost in thoughts of Cameron, Cami, and Zac. It was like they were all taking two steps forward and eight steps back. Zac, probably under the logic of moving on, had somehow convinced Cami to visit Cameron with him. Knowing Cami, she had likely agreed for guilt-ridden reasons related to sleeping with him at the wedding, or because her competitive streak wouldn't allow her to be one-upped in the forgiveness game by Zac adding Cameron's picture to the tribute wall at the restaurant. Or, maybe she had done it simply to make Mrs. Greene happy. Carolyn had gently prodded both Zac and Cami to forgive Cameron since his second suicide attempt years ago.

Kate shuddered at the darkness of those days. It was New Year's Eve and she herself was in treatment confronting her own rock bottom and preparing to reenter the real world. She remembered walking into a visitation room, surprised to see her father and Cami. It had been weigh-in day and she'd left her hair as oily as possible and wet it in the middle of a messy bun to exaggerate her progress. They always weighed them naked, or she would have worn extra socks and underwear as well. At this point, every ounce still counted to get back to her life.

"Hi, baby," her father had said in a hoarse voice tapping his left thumb against the golden cufflink on his right wrist.

"Hi, Daddy," she'd smiled, feeling like a child who'd just been pardoned from a chore. Cami hadn't said a word and stood stoically by the window, her stormy expression clashing with the sunny garden scenes on the drapes. And in an instant, Kate had realized why they were there. "What's wrong? What's he done?"

"Kate, let's all sit down." The counselor's hand was on her shoulder, guiding her to the chair opposite of her father.

"Just tell me," she'd begged. "Cami, what's he done?"

"He tried it again." Cami had said without emotion, still staring out the window.

"What? How?"

"The how doesn't matter, baby."

"Is he—?"

"No, but he is in critical condition. He was deprived of oxygen for quite a while, and if he recovers his cognitive abilities will be much less than they were before."

"And the disfigurement?"

"It's the same, baby. No worse. Your mother wanted to tell you after you finished your treatment, and if he pulled through, but I thought you deserved to know. So did Camille."

"Does Mother know you're here?"

"She does."

"Kate," the counselor interrupted softly. "We all trust that you can handle this. And we are all here to see you through it."

She said more about recovery and rituals and privileges and preparation, but Kate felt like she was underwater and caught only every other word.

"Can I have a moment? Alone, please? I need to process everything."

"Of course, baby."

She looked up into her father's face and noticed how aged he was for his fifty years. He was as well dressed as he had always been, but there was a slack to his waistline and a drawn look to his jaw. He bent to kiss her on the head as he always did and she noticed the broken vessels in his eyes and the wispy hairs covering the pink patch of skin that seemed to be puddling on top of his head.

"Thank you, Daddy. For telling me."

"Cami." Her words failed her and she didn't know what to say except that she knew Cami had been right to tell her dad that she was slipping into old habits and that she was sorry she had screamed at her and hadn't called on her birthday.

"Do you want me to stay?"

"Please."

The whispered word had been their bridge and when they were alone, Kate had finally let her anger at her brother loose on Cami's shoulder and told her how guilty she felt that her best friend was the one sitting here hurt again by her brother.

"He's not a bad person," she'd choked out, "he just doesn't have anyone. Not even me. He's lost everything. Blane. Zac. His future. Everything but our screwed-up parents."

"I'm not here to talk about Cameron's problems. I'm here because I care about you. You're better than this. Get healthy and let's move on together. That was the plan, remember?"

"I will. I am. Cami, hear me though. Hear me when I say I'm sorry. I feel responsible for what Cameron did and for all the pain my family has caused to you and the Greenes."

"I know you do. I don't know what to tell you to change that except that I'm still here. I'm still showing up for you." She'd jabbed her chin into her shoulder and added, "And I still need you. So, get better, dammit, so we can deal with this nightmare together."

They'd both broken a bit in that moment of sheer honesty and, much like a scab that falls from a wound when its job is done, begun to trust the strength in their scars. Twenty minutes later, her father was gone and she and Cami were back in her room staring at each other over a cafeteria tray.

"They treat me like I'm a doll on a shelf here."

"Well, you do kind of look like a porcelain shell of a person."

"Ha, ha. I said I'm working on it." She took an enormous bite of hummus from her plastic plate and asked. "See? Now, tell me what Cameron did."

"Kate, no."

"The counselors always say the more we're sheltered, the more we'll hide under our disease when we get out. Tell me what he did. I'd rather hear it from you than from anyone else."

"Fine. No one knows exactly how, but he managed to fish a nail file out of either your mother or your grandmother's purse when they visited. He cut his sedative drip after they left and tied the piping to the spokes of the bed and around his neck, then pushed forward on the bed wheels until it tightened like a noose. They don't know how long he was unconscious."

Mother probably gave it to him, Kate remembered thinking. A divot in the asphalt bounced the stroller roughly and she bent to the side to steal a peek at Liam. Thankful he was still asleep, Kate picked up her pace and changed directions toward Zac's café. It was her turn to save Cami from herself.

Cami

She wasn't as interested in him in the mornings, which was convenient given his propensity for cuddling after they had sex. Cami didn't do clingy, and no amount of arousal was going to make her miss her run or be late for work to listen to Zac idealize what a step forward the night before hadn't been. He chattered incessantly in the mornings about his day ahead at the café only to inevitably say he hoped she would come by for dinner, or meet him out somewhere. It was these moments that told her what they would never be in the light of day.

Ellie

Ellie stood out of view at the top of the stairs listening to the hushed conversation between Patrick and Mathilda below. She hated not having her own space to retreat to.

"She had a right to know, Patrick. She has a life to plan."

"Yes, but you weren't the one to tell her. Just because moving home is what you want for me doesn't mean it's what's best. You have to give me time. I don't know if I want to be in the States, but I do know I want to be with Ellie."

"Then let me go apologize. I know it was wrong, but you're my son and I don't feel like I've taken a single breath since I watched you almost murdered on that dreadful carpet! You will understand when you're a fath—."

Ellie shuddered as the ramification of the stalled word tumbled out of Mathilda's mouth ahead of the last syllable.

"Then again, maybe you won't."

"Goodnight, Mum."

"But you've always wanted children."

"Yet another conversation best left to Ellie and I, in the future, when the time is right. Goodnight."

Ellie listened to the front door close and pulled out her phone.

I New Text: To Jess Cell

Pride and Prejudice? Stage version? London? Grayson/
Barrett? Tell me why I didn't know.

Reply: From Jess Cell

Because Blythe didn't want you to. I was respecting my
client's wishes.

Reply: To Jess Cell

Your clients are my clients. You work for me.

Reply: From Jess Cell

I used to.

What?!? Ellie's left hand flew into the air in disbelief. Did Jess just quit?
Her fingers whirred over the screen as if they were chasing a life raft
upstream.

Reply: To Jess Cell

Please talk to me before you do anything rash. I deserve
the chance to counter.

Her screen stayed silent as she walked into Pat's room, considering
whether to leave on the next flight to appease Jess or to hire her replace-
ment. She had teleconferenced with her vice president of PR just yesterday and he had given no indication that this kind of restructure was
on the horizon. Her instincts told her this was about power for Jess. She
opened her airline app and pressed the concierge tab. The real question

was could Jess be wooed to stay and, if so, was it wise for Ellie to let her? In many ways, she was grooming a future competitor.

"Ellie?"

She jumped and turned to see Pat standing winded in the doorway wearing the same apologetic expression he had worn when he scared her on her patio during their first night together.

"Can I say I'm sorry? I don't know how what should have been a celebratory evening disintegrated into such a disaster."

"I don't know where to start, Pat. I jumped into your world with both feet, thinking we were here for treatment and respite. I don't understand why you kept this from me when we've bared our souls about so much else. It hurts that you never planned to tell me before I left."

"That's not exactly true. I just didn't want to bring up such a mammoth conversation until I was sure it was what I wanted. I only found out this morning, right before our quarrel over dingbat Marcus."

"Who else knows?"

"My mum, clearly," he said with a roll of his eyes. "My dad, my brother, and Blythe. Look, Ellie," he shuffled to the corner of the bed and eased himself down, losing control two inches before the mattress and landing with a thud. Sweat dotted his brow and the muscles in his forearm trembled on the handle of the cane. "Please don't take this as me making a life-altering decision without you. I haven't even seen the full script yet or met the director. My intent was to go back to Los Angeles for the Globes and see if I could reconcile my fear."

The veiled exertion in his voice and the underlying ache to capture what you could of a life spinning out of control tempered her anger and she went to him, silencing her buzzing phone and placing it on the nightstand.

"I'm furious that my mum spilled the beans about the offer. It was a shock you certainly didn't need. I would promise she's not always this insufferable, but I would be lying."

"She loves you and wants you safe. I can't fault her there."

"It's more than that. Did you hear the first thing she said after the nomination?"

"About never getting you to Oxford now?"

"Yes."

He clenched his jaw in unspoken pain and Ellie guided him back onto the pillows lining the headboard.

"Thank you. I think the, um, various excitements have done me in. Anyway, she is like a dog with a bone when she believes she's right. Oxford equals respectability. Acting is not a career; it's a hobby. The sciences are my true destiny. If you must give up university, the theatre trumps film. Just once, I would like to see what I *have* accomplished be acknowledged instead of what I haven't."

"That's all understandable. I guess my first question is do you want to play Mr. Darcy?"

"I won't lie. It's tempting. Then again, I'm not sure I want to make my return to the stage in something so iconic."

"Then let me wear both hats—publicist and girlfriend—for a minute and ask what kind of money is behind this production? I don't think I need to tell you what the purists will say about an American, especially Blythe Barrett, playing Elizabeth Bennet. Modern re-telling or not. It's a risk."

"I don't think they are the intended audience. It's a reimagining for a younger crowd."

"You mean the all-grown-up-with-disposable-income *Destiny* fans? The millennials who still despise the character Blythe played for dumping their teenaged heartthrob Lucas Lucien on screen, and the *real* Blythe for cheating on you? Without a gargantuan marketing budget behind this production, you might be better off with the purists."

"That's an excellent point." He arched his back and let a long breath out of his nose.

"How's your pai—"

"Manageable," he interrupted in his best lying voice. "These are the exact questions I planned to answer before I worried you with it. I don't even know if the director wants me or if he's just humoring Blythe. On the flip side, it would be fun to play opposite of each other again. This is her dream role. Did you know she owns a first edition of every cover of Pride and Prejudice that has ever been printed? I once bid on a replica of Austen's family bookcase at Smithby's as an annive—err, as a gift."

"Thoughtful."

Ellie ruffled his hair into his face, not liking the surge of jealousy churning in the pit of her stomach over what had been given to and enjoyed by a different lover who never had to trouble her young beautiful self with tracking his cryotherapy, nightmares, and muscle spasms. Pat grimaced again and she reached for her phone to call the nurse for heavier pain meds and finish changing her flight.

Leila

"Try to contain your silence," Leila joked and her class laughed. "We understand their motivations, but the question remains—what is mercy? When is deception a kindness? Hemingway thrusts his characters into lose-lose situations and demands they, and in turn the reader, answer for man's basest elements and original sins."

Leila scribbled the arc of a Plutonic dialogue across the smart board, loving the rush of being back in the classroom.

"Do we lie to be kind and spare feelings, or is it to save ourselves from the discomfort that telling the truth would cause?"

She would leave here and go straight to daycare to pick up the girls, then spend the afternoon with them, grade papers during their screen time, heat up leftovers, and put them to bed before the babysitter got there. It was date night and she and Wes were finally going to see *Life of Us*.

Kate

ate thanked the blond hostess for finding a place to park Liam's wheels among the ergonomic plastic rainbow of jogging strollers, all bursting with colorful yoga mats in slings, and took in the mélange of patrons in the packed café. Runners stretched and patted each other on the back in line for the juice bar while suited professionals raised espresso cups to their lips, tapping screens and passing paperwork back and forth. A long L-shaped table of mothers chatting and pinching off bits of fruit and pastries for babies in highchairs wound around the curve of the back wall.

"Are you with the moms club?"

"Definitely not," Kate answered more sharply than she'd meant to. She held Liam a little closer to her chest. "I'm actually here to see Zac."

"Mr. Prescott? The owner? "

"Yes."

"Are you the Golden Vintners' vendor?" She flipped through the tablet in her hand.

"No. Just please tell him Kate Stone is here and would like to speak with him for a few minutes when he has a free moment."

"Um. Okay. Let me go find him." She passed the tablet to another blond hostess and picked up the walkie-talkie on the podium. Kate took a seat on the bench near the door, admiring the burlap coffee sacks the designer had combed and finished into upholstery.

"Are you serious? I have four people waitlisted for that two-top." The other blond replied.

"He said first available."

"Fine. He better be her baby daddy from the looks I'm about to get." She yanked a menu from behind the podium and walked to Kate. "Right this way. Will you be needing a chair for the baby?"

"Yes, please." Kate adjusted the diaper bag on her shoulder, feeling like every eye in the room was on her and her table for one and a half.

"Mr. Prescott is meeting with the PM prep line crew and will be out shortly. Can I ask your waitress to start you with a cappuccino or a mimosa?"

Still warm from her run, Kate considered ordering a cold-pressed juice the size of her son, but couldn't bring herself to accept the sugars and settled for iced black coffee instead. A congenial busboy brought a slick white highchair and a bento box of house-made brown rice puffed cereal, steamed peas, and diced bananas to the table. Kate pulled a sanitizing wipe out of her diaper bag and wiped the straps before buckling him in and spreading a few of the airy occupying puffs in front of him. She watched him paw at the cereal on the tray and coo as they stuck to his wet hands.

"Almost, buddy. Keep trying!" she encouraged, catching one of the mothers at the large table watching her. They were probably saying he wasn't old enough for every fifth puff that made it to his mouth.

"Are my people taking good care of you?"

Kate looked up to see Zac's huge grin stretched between the dimples that had always kept him looking years younger than he actually was.

"They certainly are," she said, realizing that the coffee had arrived without her noticing.

"And look at this little guy! He's getting so big! Did you drive your mom here?" Liam squealed in answer and reached up to him.

"I know. Leila always says the days are long and the years are short and she couldn't be more right. Sometimes, I swear he's bigger at bedtime than he was that morning."

"That's because your arms are twice as tired," he laughed.

Kate took a fabric sensory book from her diaper bag and handed it to Liam. She didn't want him to get into the habit of only entertaining himself with food.

"Good point." She stirred a half a packet of stevia into her coffee, not sure where to start the conversation she had come to have.

"I know I make the best iced java in town, but there has to be another reason you're here. Is it Cameron?"

"Partly. I want to talk about Cami. I know you've been visiting him together."

"I know I should have told you. I'm just trying to help us all finally move on—Cameron included. When Mrs. Greene finally convinced Cami she needed to visit him in the interest of closure, I went as a buffer."

"Why you? Why not ask me?"

His brown eyes poured into hers like she should already know the answer.

"Because it's the only way she lets me spend time with her. Or it was in the beginning anyway. What else did she tell you?"

"I know you're sleeping together. I don't think that's healthy for either one of you."

"It's more than that. Did she tell you I came to her at the track on the night of Gracie's wedding? That I asked for the Greene family's blessing to pursue her?"

Kate stared across the table at him as Liam threw his book to the floor. Zac picked it up like it was second nature and scooped some peas onto the tray, never taking his eyes off of Kate.

"It wasn't ever going to be a one night stand for me. Not only am I in love with her, but I am also literally the only person who can love her like he would have wanted her to be loved. Tell me who else can shoulder his loss with her every single day better than I can? Much less honor his memory with her like I will?"

"But that's not what she's doing. She's not moving on to something new with you. She's just pretending you're him."

"For now. But not forever. She's making progress. Last night, for example, she was particularly on edge after Ellie's and she let me hold her while we talked. It's going to take time, but I am willing to wait."

"She won't, Zac. She's using this 'friends with benefits' thing you've got going on to live in her memories. Think about it. Do you ever sleep in her bed? You don't. No one ever has but Blane. In *eleven* years. She takes lovers from time to time, but it's always this way. Casual dates, if any at all, and zero intimacy."

"Like I said, she's making progress. She'll see me as more eventually, on her terms. And, until then, I'll wait."

"You don't know her like I do. She's making love to a memory, not to you."

"What if that's enough for me?"

"You can't be serious."

"I am, Kate. She's the one. That's why it's never worked for either of us with anyone else. We're meant to be together and if that means she sees Blane sometimes when she closes her eyes, then that's what I have to accept. Every partner comes with some kind of price."

"You're so wrong that I don't even know where to begin, Zac. You deserve more than being his stand in."

"I guess that's a penance I am willing to pay. She'll come around. We'll start to really move on and she'll finally see what we could be together."

"She won't." Kate lowered her tone to almost a whisper. "Not unless you make it harder for her to pretend."

"Then tell me what do. I won't end it."

"For starters, ditch the Eternity."

"My cologne?"

"You and Blane both wore it in college. She still sprays her sheets with it."

"Done. What next?"

"Don't let her stay stagnant. Make her be in public with you. No more between the sheets dates without dinner and conversation first. I'll work on her from my side. Ken will help."

Kate ignored the gratitude on his face, fully aware she had just ended Cami's affair.

Norah

1 New Text: To Leila Cell

Total waste of time. Matt just wants to hear me catalogue my sins.

Reply From: Leila Cell

Sorry I missed this. I was teaching. Sounds awful. You ok?

1 New Text: To Leila Cell

Not really. My life is a mess. The only perk to back to back no shows is stealing a catnap at my desk.

Thankful for the reprieve, Norah put her phone into the top drawer of her desk and leaned back in her chair.

She began the restful mind meditation she had learned years ago in Mumbai when the heat made it impossible to sleep no matter how exhausted she was.

1 New Text From: Leila Cell

True confession...I think I agreed to therapy with my mom for the wrong reasons. I don't know why I thought it could help before it's too late. She and Tanya gang up on me every time and I leave feeling like the most selfish person who ever lived.

Norah was slipping into her third visualization when a sharp rap on her door followed by Ashlynn's desperate voice yanked her back into the bright fluorescents of her office.

"Jillan needs you in room 4. We just checked Dr. Blieger's patient and she is nearly crowning."

Norah flew up from her desk and raced with Ashlynn down the hallway.

"This is Dr. Merrit," Jillan said squatted on the stool.

Norah washed her hands at lightening speed and slipped them into Ashlynn's outstretched gloves. The patient looked frantically from her to Jillan to Ashlynn who was now laying out the emergency instruments they might need.

"I, I didn't know. I never doubled over or nothing like I done with the last three. My boyfriend always says I could talk through a root canal and may-iiiiiiiiiiyyyybeee," she gasped in pain, "he's riiiiiyght."

"You're doing great. In fact, you're making this look a little too easy."

Norah kept eye contact with the patient and placed her hand firmly on the straining perineum.

"Don't tell our other patients, okay?" she said squatting to take Jillan's place on the stool and listening for the heavy footsteps of the EMTs' boots to break the silence in the hallway.

Ellie

1 New Text: From Mathilda Grayson

My dear, I am so very sorry for my behaviour this evening. Please forgive me. It's only that if my sixty years have taught me anything, it's that everything can wait. Nothing trumps time with those we love. Again, I am terribly sorry.

It can wait. She looked over at sleeping Pat and ached to stay as much as she ached to go.

Pat's eyes flew open and she thought again about the nightmare she could be living if the bullet had entered or exited two inches differently.

"Blythe!" He called, but reached for Ellie without fully waking and she thought of the nightmare she would be living if her firm collapsed because she had risked it all on a man.

Cami

"What's all this?" Cami asked as she walked into Zac's darkened living room and breathed in the heavy scent of lavender.

"It's a surprise. Meet Misha."

He nodded across the room at a stern looking woman locking the legs of a massage table into position.

"I have a standing appointment with her every Monday to recover from my weekend training and asked her to make tonight's session for two."

"You know I'm kind of a sure bet. You don't need to loosen me up."

Cami flung her windbreaker over the edge of his sofa, irritated that he was drawing the evening out.

"You might be, but who says I am?" he grinned.

"Track record." Cami cracked her neck, deciding to humor him before bedding him and going home to sleep.

"Vee begin now. Thees isss my parrrrdtner, Stephania. She vill work on you and I on your girl. We vill turn around vhile you deesrobe. Meester Prescottt knows zee ageeenda." Misha's thick Slavic accent rose and fell with the candlelight that flickered on the ceiling.

"You're different tonight." Cami took off her shirt and sports bra as one and whipped the pair onto the windbreaker. Zac said something she didn't quite catch and she crawled under the warmed sheet. "What?"

"I said you really don't get foreplay, do you?"

"That's not what this is."

"It could be."

"Maybe you're just paying attention to the wrong area." She pressed her face into the padded donut.

"And you said you didn't need to be loosened up."

"Now vee are quiet." Misha's ultimatum was a relief to Cami.

"I like deep tissue."

"You suck."

"I what?" She raised her head in time to hear Zac chuckle.

"Your socks." He said through stifled laughter.

"Yes. You socks. Take zem off like Meester Prescott. My hands don't like to be eenterroopted."

Cami knew she had heard her correctly the first time, but obliged and quickly wondered if Misha had learned her technique from the KGB as her fingers turned to iron and she proceeded to pound every fiber of Cami's back into submission.

Leila

"Oh my God, Wes. I am so sick of your bowels I could scream!"

"I'm sorry, babe. I can't help it."

"Seriously? You can't help it? You wouldn't walk into anyone's office and do that. You wouldn't do it in the middle of a meeting or while you were with a client, so why do you think it's okay to do it walking into our bedroom? Sheesh. It's like I don't even matter."

Leila flipped the duvet down on her side of the bed. It was bad enough that he'd been too late to make their dinner reservation and she had sat at the restaurant bar by herself grading papers, but then he had taken at least three calls during what was quite possibly the most romantic movie she had ever seen. After the movie, she had mentioned stopping for gelato, hoping they would talk about the film, but he had said he was stuffed with popcorn and wanted to go home.

"I said I was sorry."

"Twelve years together, Wes. Twelve. I've hated that since day one. You know this, but you continue to do it. What about that says I care about my wife and her feelings? Nothing."

"Okay, I'll take some Gas-X."

Leila listened to him rummaging around the medicine cabinet making a mess. There were so many things she wanted to say to him, but none of them would do any good tonight. She didn't want to fight about a fart. She wanted to be important enough for him to show up on time and be present with her.

"Babe, where's the Gas-X?"

Ugggggghhhhhhhh! Leila screamed in her mind and threw her legs over the side of the bed.

"Nevermind. I found it."

He walked out of the bathroom and headed to the kitchen like flatulence was the real problem and he had just solved it. She clicked the television on and reached for her phone.

Kate

1 New Text: To Leila Cell

How was Life of Us? Was it different seeing him on screen now that you've met him?

Reply: From Leila Cell

It was so good!!! Like-stop-your-life-and-go-now good! If he doesn't win the Golden Globe, I'll be shocked. My date sucked, but Pat made up for it ☺

1 New Text: To Leila Cell

Should have taken me. LOL. I could look at him all day long. Why was your date bad?

Reply: From Leila Cell

Same old, same old. I am not a big enough dot on Wes' radar to warrant three hours of his time. He missed dinner.

I sat at the bar by myself and graded papers. Then, he kept leaving during the movie to take work calls. I wanted to go somewhere after and actually talk to each other and he wanted to come home where he spent the rest of our evening passing gas and I tried and failed not to bite his head off for being inconsiderate. He knew how much I was looking forward to tonight.

I New Text: To Leila Cell

I'm sorry. Wouldn't it be nice to just be dated again? Like it was their idea?

Reply: From Leila Cell

From your mouth to God's ears.

I New Text: To Leila Cell

At least you have a decent sex life the other six days of the week. I'm still spending most of our time in the bedroom avoiding my husband.

Reply: From Leila Cell

LOL. You'll get back to it. It just takes practice after baby. Think of it like running. The less you do it, the less you want to.

I New Text: To Leila Cell

So, you want to go for a run? I'll come pick you up.

Kate added the crying laughing face emoji and immediately received the puking emoji and a GIF of Phoebe from *Friends* freewheeling through Central Park in response.

Kate smiled and sat her fading phone on the charging base before it died completely. Leila and Wes's ruts were always short lived. They would be back to happy in a day or two, whereas she and Ken seemed to have taken up permanent residence in the land of meh. It wasn't that she was unhappy. If anything, watching him be everything and more she could want in a father for Liam had tripled her feelings for him. And it wasn't that she didn't miss their pre-baby love making as much as he did. It was that, at the end of the day, she longed for a calm, autonomous, few hours without someone needing her body. Thankfully, tonight was Ken's fantasy football draft, which would keep him in the living room, glued to his laptop, and she could watch HGTV in peace.

Norah

"Now, *that* is a day," Evelyn said over speakerphone as Norah sat on the bed, towel drying her hair and hoping that one day her child would feel the same calm hearing her voice that she still felt talking to her mother. "Do you want me to bring you some dinner?"

"I'm in the room now, eagerly awaiting my forty dollars worth of Chinese for one to arrive."

"So, you're alone? I didn't want to pry."

"Yes, I'm alone. Alone. Lonely. Pregnant. Exhausted. Confused. Torn between two men. Your daughter is pretty much a walking Lifetime movie."

"You can always come home."

"I know, but I think I'll hold on to my last shred of dignity."

"Understandable," Evelyn snickered.

"But, thanks for the offer. It's nice to know it's there in a pinch."

"Of course, honey. I am glad you and Matt are talking to someone. I truly am, but please be careful about what you chase."

"I'm not chasing him, Mom. I'm just not ready to write off our marriage completely. Hence the therapy."

"I didn't mean him. I meant make sure you're chasing the life you want."

The truth in her mother's words attached itself to Norah's heart like a weight and dragged it to the pit of her stomach.

"Honey? Did I lose you?"

"Okay, Mom."

There was a knock at the door.

"Listen, I need to go." Norah took the phone off of speaker and sandwiched it between her ear and shoulder as she walked to the table by the door and fished a dollar bill out of her purse.

"Are you upset?"

"No, Mom. My food is here."

She turned the top deadbolt and pulled the handle in a motion that had become as routine as opening the lock to the on-call room at the hospital.

"Special delivery?"

Enrique lifted a plastic bag emblazoned with the Royal Pagoda restaurant's logo into the air, looking impossibly crisp in white shorts and a heather gray Polo shirt. Norah stood in the doorway, not sure whether seeing him eased or intensified the racket in her brain.

"Norah?"

Evelyn's voice shook her to attention and she raised a finger to her lips.

"Sorry. Love you, more. I'll call you sometime tomorrow. Goodbye."

Enrique raised an eyebrow at the dollar bill in her hand. "Has anyone ever told you that you're a lousy tipper?"

"Come in. Do I even want to know how this happened?"

"Fate."

"I am too tired to think that's cute."

"I'm serious. I was in line to pay our bill at Royal Pagoda and the cashier was taking your order. I heard your name, your favorites, and the room number, so I came here and waited for the delivery guy."

"Our bill?"

"I was with my girls. I'm going to pick them up from soccer practice every Tuesday night and take them to dinner. When I'm settled, they'll start spending the night."

"I'm sorry," Norah said, losing her appetite. "It's been a Monday of a Tuesday."

"It was a fair question." He unloaded the cartons out of their cardboard holder and put them on the table. "Why don't you get in bed and let me take care of you?"

Exhaustion and her ache for his touch taunted her resolve and she glanced at the perfectly turned-down, pillowed, euphoria of the crisp white comforter.

"Enrique, I can't."

"Can't what? Eat?"

Enrique's eyes danced as he held up the makeshift bed tray he had concocted from the cardboard holder. He draped the paper napkin over his arm and placed the opened cartons side by side, each sprouting its own set of chopsticks.

"Haven't you heard of Netflix and chill?"

Norah laughed at such a hip phrase coming out of someone so preppy and slid under the sheets.

"Just chilling? Huh?"

"Yes. I want to be with you and that's going to mean there are days like these and nights when you need rest. I can be that for you in ways that I never was for Deanna."

"And help me raise another man's child?"

"If that's what it takes."

"But it's not what you want."

"I have three children, Norah. Deanna wanted one more and I want a vasectomy. It's something we fight, fought, about constantly. "

"And if it's yours by a fluke of latex?"

"Then we'll name him 'junior.'"

Norah pushed a sip of the egg drop soup on her tray past the lump that was still in her throat.

"What if I want another child in the future?"

"Why borrow trouble? You haven't even changed your millionth diaper yet."

"I'm serious, Enrique. Is it something you would consider?"

"If it kept me with you, I might."

"Then we'll table it. No surgeries."

"What about 'my body, my choice?'"

He snatched a baby corn from her stir-fry and clicked on the television. Norah ate a few bites more before falling asleep where she sat, waking only briefly when he took the tray he had made from her lap and turned off the lights.

Leila

"I'm so glad we can come here more often now that I'm closer." Leila bounced Liam on her lap and checked the time on her phone. Zac's lunch specials were definitely a perk of the commute to the university.

"Me, too. It's our new favorite run." Kate said, distracted by something over Leila's shoulder, and dicing a kiwi slice into segments. She stopped her reach just as Liam grabbed at it. "Wait, when can they have kiwi?"

"Six months? Nine months? I have forgotten so much!"

Liam giggled and tugged at her necklace.

"Did you know there's an app for introducing foods now?"

"Of course there is." Leila clapped Liam's hands together and soaked up the delicious baby laugh that followed.

"How was the rest of the night with Wes?"

"I fell asleep before he came to bed and he was gone when I woke up. I swear he could have a secret life and I would never know."

"Yeah, but that would require time. He gets the same twenty-four hours as the rest of us."

"Speaking of affairs, two of the professors in my department are divorcing their spouses of twenty years to marry each other. One of their wives caught on and hired a PI to follow them on a research trip."

"Wow. That's insane," Kate replied absently, still watching something over Leila's shoulder. "While we're discussing affairs, does Zac seem extra antsy today, or is it just my imagination?"

"I hadn't noticed. Then again, before I went back to work I only came here on bench day."

"If he is, he has good reason to be. I did something."

"What? Wait, I don't think I'm following."

"I couldn't stop thinking about Cami's revelation at Ellie's, so I did something to stop it."

"To stop her and Zac?"

"Yes. Ken said I was out of line, but I think it's for the best."

Liam threw his pacifier to the floor and Kate pushed half of her untouched egg whites to the opposite side of her plate. Leila bent and grabbed it, thinking she did not miss the baby phase after all as Kate dug for a wipe and began to clean it. With Clara, she would have done the same. With Julia, she would have simply wiped it on her napkin and handed it back to her.

"Help me understand. They aren't doing anything wrong. I wouldn't call it an affair, exactly."

"But it is for Cami. She's dissatisfied with her life and using him as a vehicle to re-live what she had with Blane. Zac thinks that's temporary, but I know it's not. Cami will jog in place with him for the rest of their lives if he lets her."

"So, what did you do?"

"I told him to shake her out of it and to make her actually see him for him, date him, and be a part of his life."

"I'm no fan of the friends with benefits act, but what if that's their foundation? Why not let it run its course and grow into a bigger connection than their grief?"

"Because it won't! He will wait for her forever unless he knows there's no chance she'll ever see him as more than an escape!"

"Okay," Leila stalled, surprised at Kate's volume. "I will readily admit that my mind doesn't work the same way that Cami's does, but I don't think she is trying to be hurtful. Zac is part of her memories, too. Whatever she has with him clearly feels good to her, so why interfere?"

"Believe me, Leila, if she was any bit in love with him we wouldn't be having this conversation. What I did was an intervention of sorts." Liam fussed and arched his back. Leila supported him under his arms and helped him stand on her thighs, checking his diaper out of habit.

"I still don't know what you did," she said, both anxious to know and to leave early enough to find parking in the faculty lot.

"I told him she was using him and would continue to until he made her consider him as a potential partner and not as a stand-in for Blane. He thinks he's perfect for her because he understands what she's lost. He is literally willing to accept being the second love of her life. I think he's a grieving fool, but deserves more than she can give."

"That's, um, complicated. In some ways, I see his point. Strong feelings are strong feelings. It still sounds like the beginning of a relationship to me. You know, when the blinders are on and you can't see the other person's flaws. Cami isn't great at vulnerability, so maybe it's a good thing that she knows his drawbacks from the beginning. Sometimes, I think the reason Wes and I work is because we fell in love with each other's drive to succeed just as much as we did with each other."

"Maybe you're right." Kate reached for Liam as he arched his back again. "But Zac is one of the good ones and Cami will break his heart."

"Maybe she won't. Couldn't this be her version of happy?"

"No."

Ellie

Pat dismissed Ellie's third request to take a cab to the airport. "They'll follow you anyway."

"I know," she said, acknowledging the paparazzi who had resumed their vigil outside his home since the Globe nominations. "I love that you want to take me. I really do, but it makes discretion so much harder and Dominic doesn't report back until Monday."

"Screw discretion, let your fellow take ya' to the airport." The nurse said loudly as she took his pressures. "Heathrow could use a little excitement."

"See? She's on my side."

"So, the man who doesn't want to go back to LA because of visibility, wants to shake things up by popping into Heathrow for a quick goodbye?"

Ellie kissed his forehead, scanning the room one last time to make sure she hadn't forgotten anything.

"Maybe that's 'er plan. Make you miss 'er a little."

"Maybe I already do." He said it directly to Ellie and handed her an envelope from his shirt pocket. "At least let me give you something to read on the plane."

His grin brought her focus back to him and she registered, again, how much she would miss this. The room seemed to freeze for a moment and she took in the white cable-knit sweater he was wearing and memorized the way his eyes crinkled when he smiled.

"Are you all right, love?"

"I'm fine." Ellie looked away as Pat asked the nurse to step out. Every breath she took seemed to burn her eyes and she wanted nothing more than to crawl into his lap and kiss him one more time. Before she could move, his arms circled her waist and he pulled her to his chest.

"I was so focused on packing that I forgot I was really going home for a moment."

"This is us, Ellie. This is how we say goodbye."

"It's just that I'm not ready. I can't stay and I don't want to leave."

"You're going back to something you love."

"The American Dream." She brushed her lips against his neck, lingering over the warmth. "I built it from the ground up and now I get to work until I die to keep it."

"It worries me seeing you this cynical, Ellie."

"I have to go." The words left her lips more a command than a statement and she squeezed his hand one last time.

Cami

Cami listened to the laughter coming through the wall and stared at the art allotment proposals in front of her. Twelve hours per frame for the next shoot, not including editing and artistic effort? They were clearly mocking her prediction requests.

She opened her mailbox and created a group message. If they chose not to make relevant contributions, they chose not to be part of the conversation. The phrase *unable to communicate goals effectively to support staff* had been the most insulting on the exit paperwork from InFocus. Seventeen teams had answered to her for the last eight years. She'd naively assumed the profit margin she produced and the bonuses she received from her bosses spoke volumes for her "communication" skills.

CC: Dean Gatz
BCC: camiandblane42299@aol.com

Upon review of the allotment proposals you submitted (see attached), it is clear the design team is 100 percent in agreement that they require more time for the shoot than for editing. Therefore, I have readjusted the design schedule for the next two projects. Each artist shall have twelve hours to shoot the vehicles and sculptures on loan.

Those hours shall not be included in the prediction and need not be documented. Artists will then submit to me the shots they feel are most promising. I will then review, discuss, and assign an editing schedule to ensure we meet our deadlines.

Ms. Camille Clark
Creative Director
Gatz, Ferris, and Hart Productions

Cami reached into her desk for her spare Jaybuds as she closed her computer and turned her chair toward the window. She would give herself a ten-minute break now, instead of having taken a lunch fifteen minutes ago. She selected today's *Fresh Air* podcast and shut her eyes. At this time of day, LA's skyline was more like the poster child for global warming than a marker of corner-office success.

Terry Gross's rhythmic voice filled her ears midsentence. "Would you say you crave normalcy?"

"Absolutely," a British voice answered. "Then again, I feel guilty admitting so. The immediate thing that comes to mind is the throng of serious actors behind me who also wanted the role. Those kids would give anything to have lived my distorted version of reality during the craziest of the *Destiny* days, or even at the present moment."

"So, you don't consider yourself serious?"

"Well, I wasn't then. I was just a model with a few commercials under my belt who answered an open-call advertisement I saw in the Thursday paper. The kids I am talking about had been tapping their hearts out for dance and talent agents since they were six years old and vying for every role under twenty in the West End for years. Whilst I knew without doubt that acting was what I wanted to spend my life doing, I didn't exactly have the freedom to pursue it as a serious profession."

"Is it true you decided to forgo a scholarship to Oxford just to make the callback?"

"The final one, yes. The initial three, no. The date conflicted with a mandatory orientation week for all entering freshers, and I chose to go to LA for the final audition. Passing on the scholarship was one of the most difficult decisions I've ever made—and the scariest, mind you. My family was none too happy about it, but I followed my dream. Scratch that. I should preface this all by saying it was also the stupidest thing I've ever done. I don't want any of the teenagers listening to use their college application cash for a bus ticket to audition for *Idol* or the like."

"But your gamble paid off."

"Some would say that's still being decided, but yes. I had only a laughable professional résumé and a modeling portfolio one second, and a sharp-dressed man offering me tickets to California to read with Blythe the next."

"What did it feel like to walk into that room as one of the final ten for the role?"

"I'd like to say it felt great, but it didn't. It felt…"

He paused, and Cami remembered squirming in the waiting room of her design school entrance interview as she surveyed the slick leather portfolios of her bohemian-chic competition and realized she was the only one carrying a plastic three-ring binder of prints. It was the last time she ever overlooked something as crucial as packaging before presenting her work. As for the ill-fitting khakis and Scrunchie she wore, Kate took care of that after they met.

"It felt like I was this big impostor and even if I did make it past the other hopefuls, I'd always be known as the long shot who stumbled into something iconic by sheer luck for the rest of my career."

"My research shows four of your last five films opened at number one and grossed record audiences worldwide, so why veer off that path now with something as minimalist as *Life of Us*?"

"Understand that I mean no disrespect to those roles. They were all challenging in their own ways, and I learned loads about the craft from my co-stars and directors, but I wanted to do something different, something timely that spoke to the civil rights and humanitarian work left to do around the world. Western society is making loads of progress regarding marriage equality whilst Uganda and other countries legalize murder based solely upon sexuality."

"This is Terry Gross, and you're listening to *Fresh Air*. When we return, Patrick Grayson and I will discuss the accolades and outrage surrounding his latest film, *Life of Us*, the questions it begs, and the implications it places upon us all about our legacies."

Cami had heard enough and deleted the podcast. If he was playing with her friend, she hoped he knew he was playing with fire. Ellie did a lot of things well, but forgiveness wasn't one of them. Marcus was living proof.

Cami pitied anyone who dared mess with Ellie's success after that debacle. She had come back from Cinque Terre as a woman determined—possessed, rather—to rebuild her reputation. Cami and the others had watched her work like a madwoman to claw her way back to the top of the PR world. But when she got there, it still wasn't enough. Even after she opened her own firm, she kept telling them she wanted to go bigger, and every time she wooed a client from Camelot or landed a new A-lister, Cami could all but see Ellie put a tally mark in the win column. There was no question that her firm was now the most sought after in LA, but she still treated every account like it might be her last. She accepted nothing but excellence from those in her employ and was as ruthlessly unforgiving of her executive publicists' mistakes as Camelot had been of hers when Marcus compromised their clients' information. That made the entire Patrick Grayson "situation" even more baffling because it was not only a repeat lapse in judgment, but extremely out of character for post-Marcus Ellie.

1 New Text: From Zac Cell

Last night was great.

Cami picked up her phone to reply and decided she had no right to judge Ellie for taking what she wanted.

Ellie

ocus, Ellie told herself as she went to the wrong side of the cab to get her bags. She thanked the driver, gave him half the tip she would have had he not cracked a joke about her hair color, and pulled her own luggage to the private security entrance.

"Ms. Lindsay! Ms. Lindsay? Ellison? Is that you?"

Ellie jerked her head toward the sound of the voice in time to see Blythe Barrett raise her oversized sunglasses and adjust her awkwardly long tee that read *I Can't Even*.

"Blythe, Hello."

Ellie changed direction and walked to where the wispy star was standing in front of a luggage cart laden with Louis Vuitton's entire spring luggage line.

"Are you leaving early? Pat said you would be here when I visited. I just arrived an hour ago."

"Only by a day." She couldn't remember if Pat had told her Blythe was coming. She had either forgotten, or Blythe was covering her bases about the *Pride and Prejudice* role she had asked Jess not to disclose. "You'll have to forgive me. I am behind on my clients' schedules. Are you here on business or pleasure?"

"Just a visit, this time, but I am hoping to make it more permanent soon."

The way she paused after 'this time' raised Ellie's guard and she let the silence stretch between them, confidant Blythe's nerves would betray her into divulging more information.

"Well, Ellison, I'm glad I saw you even if it was brief. I really don't want there to be any bad blood between us. I promise leaving your firm with Jess wasn't personal. She just gets me and I like the idea of being someone's most important client."

So that was it, Ellie thought, knowing she should have seen this coming. Jess was branching out on her own and poaching clients.

"Best of luck. I would love to see you play Elizabeth Bennett," Ellie lied.

"I didn't know you knew." Blythe rubbed the toe of her UGG boot against the cart's wheel. "I'll, um, keep our leading man company until you get back."

Kate

Kate knew she was right to protect Zac and Cami from each other even if Ken didn't think so and Leila had been skeptical. If they knew Cami as well as she did, they would agree. Kate hopped from one thought to another as she threaded Liam's favorite blanket through the harness and secured the visor a final time to protect him from the sun.

"Excuse me? Kate?"

Kate turned to see a petite woman smiling behind her.

"Me?"

"Your name is Kate, right?"

"Yes. Do I know you?" She searched the woman's hazel eyes, noticing something familiar in the purposeful messiness of the bun artfully angled on her head.

"Yes and no. We are in a," she lowered her voice, "support group together and I've seen you and your son here at the café a few times. I belong to a StrollerFit club that eats here after our workouts on Tuesdays. My one-year-old is inside with my mom, but I wanted to catch you and see if you wanted to—I don't know—chat sometime. Just the two of us. I can't speak for you, but it would do me a world of good to know another mother in recovery."

It would, Kate thought but didn't say, scared by how much she needed what this stranger was offering.

Norah

1 New Text: From Matt Cell
CC: Dr. Crinson

Assignment 1: Name a time you were proud of Norah.

We were on a camping trip with my family when my dad cut his finger to the bone fileting a fish. My mom was screaming about the blood and Faith kept trying to douse him in peroxide. Dad waved them off and insisted it was nothing. Norah managed to convince him to let her clean it and stitch him up. She did it right there by the river and he still brags about reeling in a big bass ten minutes later, good as new.

N orah remembered it, too. His family had teased her all day about it being her first camping trip and goaded Matt that his bride-to-be would starve if left to his angling abilities. She had taken their insults in stride, saying her tent was a palace compared to some of the places her missions team had slept in Mumbai and thinking Matt was putting too much emphasis on their approval. She remembered suturing his dad's thumb with her field kit and how proud Matt was that she had been useful.

Hindsight being what it was, she now understood how important that impression of her had been to Matt. She remembered trying to fit in with his family and being met with jab after jab from her future mother-in-law and sister-in-law. Though they had seen her play game after game of hopscotch with Matt's oldest niece, Kaitlin, and bait then three-year-old Christian's hook hundreds of times as he fished for perch, none of the positives mattered. Brenda and Faith only cared that she was a woman different from themselves who had to read the directions on the Bisquick box to make pancakes, and that she sat in the shade after lunch studying a new procedure she was expected to perform the following week while they collected pine cones for fall decorating. They saw nothing more than a woman who didn't define her future with the words *wife* and *mother* and who would never be good enough.

Norah picked up the lab report in front of her, scanning the patient's skyrocketing glucose levels and thinking about the rest of the camping trip. She and Matt had sat by the dying fire, cuddled under a red and green plaid blanket, drinking coffee out of tin mugs and planning the life ahead of them. When the last ember faded, they took the blanket down to the river and made love on the bank out of view of the tents. Norah remembered the earthy scent of the pine needles and the rushing sound of the water as they struggled to control their laughter at sneaking around like a pair of teenagers at summer camp. She had loved him so much then that she believed nothing and no one else would ever matter.

Reply to: Matt Cell
CC: Dr. Crinson

Thank you. On that trip, I was proud of Matt for believing in us despite his family's opinion of me.

A sharp pain ran up her jaw line and she realized she had been gritting her teeth. She closed her eyes and asked herself that if they could ever be those people again, did she want to be?

1 New Text: From Dr. Orlando Cell

How's my favorite mother to be? Can I take you to dinner?

1 New Text: To Matt Cell

Hibachi? 7:30?

1 New Text: From Matt Cell

I guess it couldn't hurt. See u there.

Ugggggghhhhhhhh! I have to stop doing that! Norah didn't know whether to laugh at herself or be furious at her fingers.

Cami

"It looks like you've got it under control, Clark. If you need anything else, you're going to have to ask it on the racquet-ball court." Dean patted his silver racquet against his leg and laughed loudly.

"Now there's an after five meeting I can get behind," Cami said turning back to her computer. "Have a good game."

"Grab your stuff and join me. We can hash out which one of these bozos are getting whacked at the quarter." He pointed his racquet toward the laughter coming from the conference room.

"I haven't played since college."

"Perfect. I like playing people who are better than me."

"Nah. I need to finish a few things and get a run in." A neon orange Nerf dart soared over the divider between her office and the conference room followed by a chorus of applause. "What the hell. Let's go pound out some frustrations and fire people."

Ellie

"**C**hampagne, Ms. Lindsay?"

"Yes, please."

Ellie took a glass from the flight attendant's tray and reclined her seat, palming her phone, and trying to shake the sinking feeling in her chest that she was leaving something behind. She thought of the glass and the card Pat had left on her kitchen island and remembered how his words took her breath away on their night in. *At least let me give you something to read on the plane.* Ellie reached into her bag and pulled out the envelope he had given her when they said goodbye. *Ms. Lindsay* was written on the front with a peculiar formality. She ran her finger under the seal and pulled out a folded piece of cardstock almost identical to the ones he had tied to the Christmas lights on her stairs. When she opened the crease, two airline tickets fell into her lap.

> *Ellison,*
>
> *This is me, still dreaming about our future and asking you to balter through it with me, fears and all. I've never wanted you to give anything up to be with me, but I see now that was an improbable wish. Loving me comes at a cost I want for no one, and for that I am deeply sorry. My life was put on hold with the pull of a trigger, and while I cannot promise you I will ever*

feel safe in the land of the free again, I can promise I won't let our story end in hospitals and behind barred English doors. You followed me into this nightmare and now it is my turn to follow you out of it. These tickets are open-ended. Tell me where to go and I am there. Somewhere we've been. Somewhere we haven't. Your choice. I have pondered staying in London endlessly, but it will never be home again. Not without you. I love you.

Missing you even as this ink dries,
Patrick Grayson

Ellie read the words a second time and looked at the empty seat beside her. She had not been this unsure of where she was going, and what was waiting for her, since her flight home from her jaunt to forget Marcus in Cinque Terre. She knew now that being alone would never be the same again. Part of her would always be with Pat, wherever he was, and part of her would always be with the first love of her life—her firm.

Norah

1 New Text: To Leila Cell

I'm not late. That's a start, right?

Of course he's not here to see it, Norah thought. She pulled the pinching waistband of her jeans lower, missing the blessed drawstring of her scrubs. Matt's place sat empty beside her as the strangers around the hibachi table sipped their cocktails and ventured introductions into each other's conversations. She busied herself looking at the menu and debating how long she should wait to vacate her seat in favor of a to-go order if he didn't show.

"And who are we waiting on here, ma'am?" The waiter asked.

"My hus—my, uh, Matt."

"Very well. Do we know what soup he would like as a starter?"

"I'm not sure. Miso?"

"Are you on a first date, too?" the strawberry-haired woman to her left asked in a bubbly voice. Norah stared blankly at her. "Because we are, and I have declared hibachi the most awkward 'meet the Tinder live' selection ever. I'm Jenny by the way."

"At least there are other people to talk to and the check is easy to split." The young man next to Jenny piped in.

"This is true." Norah chuckled.

"So who are you waiting for?" Jenny pressed.

"It's complicated."

"I went on a date once, saw the guy, and left."

"Maybe that's what happened to me." Norah smiled tightly and checked her watch. She was about to flag down the nearest kimono-clad server with the excuse that she had gotten a call and would need to abandon her reservation when a hand that was as familiar as it was foreign grazed her shoulder.

"Sorry I'm late." Matt unbuttoned his sport coat and worked himself into the space between the table and his chair.

"I think she almost gave up on you, brother." Jenny's date said extending his hand. "I'm Wallace."

"Nah, she's used to *being with* a doctor and knows the drill." Matt pumped Wallace's hand once and released it. Norah knew his word choice was a much an intentional avoidance of the word married as it was a reminder of her sin.

"I can relate! This is our *third* attempt at a first date. Wallace is always cancelling."

"Matt Merrit. It's nice to meet you." His eyes lingered on her cleavage. "Well, you had better get used to it or move on."

"That's true." Norah said half to Jenny and half to her menu.

"So, what kind of doctor are you?" Jenny asked Matt, and Norah let him squirm in his seat. "Wallace, here, is studying to be a surgeon."

"I am an attorney."

"You don't see that combo too often." Wallace added, impressed.

"You're like a total power couple."

"That's us." Matt scoffed. "Total power couple."

"What year are you, Wallace?" Norah resigned herself to making uncomfortable small talk if it meant avoiding Matt's glare.

"Fourth. Surgical."

"Ah. The Gauntlet."

"Don't I know it?" He let out a long breath while Matt helped Jenny pick a bottle of Saki from the menu.

"What's your specialty?" Wallace continued.

"I'm an OB/GYN."

"My mom is an OB."

"Oh yeah?" Matt chimed in. "Was she ever around?"

"Matt!" Norah snapped under her breath.

"Of course she was." Wallace answered awkwardly. "If you're asking if she made every little league game, she didn't. But she was always there for my sisters and me. When she was home, we had her full attention and because she was happy, our home was happy."

"You are wise beyond your years, Wallace," Norah said. "Excuse me. I seem to have lost my appetite."

She pushed her chair away from the table. . Norah caught the waiter on her way to the restroom and handed him a one hundred dollar bill to cover the soup she had ordered and asked he keep ten as tip and apply the remainder to Wallace's tab. Five minutes later she was in her car and accepting Enrique's offer of company.

$\mathscr{L}$eila

"**Y**ou can only get…"

"Better." Clara finished the Maya Angelou quote Leila used so often with her daughters and spilled directly into her next thought. "Unless you quit. Then you'll never get better. Except tying shoes doesn't count. That is *hard*."

"It won't always be. One more try and we'll say goodnight." Leila yawned.

"T-H-E- says aaaaa-m."

"Good try, sweetheart. T-H-E spells 'the.' The littlest acorn grew into the tallest oak tree."

"And that's what the story is about, too. Believing you can do some-thing even when others don't because you're different."

Clara closed the book.

"See? You've got the important part right. Everything else will come."

Leila kissed her head, reveling in the moments like this when bed-time went smoothly and motherhood wasn't throwing her new curveballs. If only her girls' problems could stay this small and solvable. She would blink and they would be teens navigating puberty and making choices, often out of her sight, that bore real consequences. She sent up a prayer that she was giving them a strong foundation and shut Clara's door. A stack of dishes waited in the sink and a pile of graded papers waited by her computer to be entered. At least angsty tweens and teens could load a dishwasher, she thought as her phone vibrated on the counter.

1 New Text: From Wes Cell

It's another late one. I know. I'm sorry about last night and I'll be home as soon as I can. We'll do family movie night or go out for pizza tomorrow. Love you.

Reply: To Wes Cell

The girls are in bed and we miss you. Tomorrow will be good for all of us. Love you, too.

The quiet house suddenly seemed colder and Leila remembered she had other homework to do tonight. She and Tanya were supposed to talk like friends. The counselor wanted them to have a conversation about anything other than their mother. She looked at the clock and saw she had missed her window and that Tanya would already be at work.

1 New Text: To Tanya Cell

I'm sorry, but I just got the girls down and realized it was too late to call. I will be up entering grades if you want to talk on your break. I apologize for losing track of time.

Reply: From Tanya Cell

Typical.

The phone works two ways. Your opinion is not my reality. Leila typed but didn't send. She knew that if the counselor's assignment had been her priority, she would have called while she made dinner or given the girls something quiet to do for twenty minutes before bed instead of painting their nails. She may have genuinely forgotten the assignment, but the truth was she didn't want to talk to Tanya and be told how selfish her choices were for the umpteenth time. Leila poured energy into the people she loved, even if they weren't her sisters by blood, and even when they didn't give the same back to her.

Cami

"Remind me not to get behind the business end of your racquet, Clark!"

Dean poured the foamy lager from the pitcher into a tilted glass and handed it to her.

"That was the most fun I've had in weeks." Cami took a long draw of the cold liquid to soothe her parched throat. "I'm glad you convinced me to go."

"Well, you looked like you needed it. I know those kids haven't made things easy for you. They can be an entitled bunch of assholes, but we need their brains."

"As much as I hate to admit it, they are pretty talented."

"I think they'll get on board with your schedules soon. They just don't see the merit yet."

"You realize we are playing 'good cop, bad cop' with them, right?"

"What do you mean? Good ol' Uncle Dean gives them compliments and late report times and mean ol' Kommandant Clark gives them zingers and deadlines?"

"Kommandant Clark? Is that what they call me?"

"I thought you knew." He laughed so loud that the group of sales-men playing darts next to them stopped their game and turned in his direction.

"I do now!" Cami plunged a tortilla chip into the ramekin of salsa on her plate. "I can't say I hate it."

"As my first wife used to say, 'it's good to be queen.'"

"First?"

"Now ex. I had two of them."

"Two ex wives?"

"No, just one. My first wife and I split when our daughter went to college. My second wife passed away two years ago next Wednesday. Breast cancer."

"I'm sorry."

"Thank you. It's not something I talk about. So, what about you? Ex-husband? Boyfriend?"

"I guess I am a widower of sorts. I don't talk about it much either."

"No fault there." Dean's voice trailed off and the noise of the pub blanketed the silence between them. "I normally wouldn't have asked, but I noticed your phone blowing up on the court and thought someone might be waiting on you at home."

"Now that's an entirely different question with an entirely more complicated answer."

I New Text: From Zac Cell

Where are you? I'm walking in to see Cameron. Should I wait?

Cami looked at the screen and pressed the star key to reject the message with an auto-reply of 'I am in a meeting.'

Norah

"So you had a passive aggressive argument in front of an audience?" Enrique said, feeding her the last spoonful of the Cherry Garcia ice cream he had brought.

"Near very sharp knives I might add."

"Yes, let's not forget there were weapons available."

"And everyone lived."

"If arguments were scored like Scrabble games, I'd say you earned a triple word score spelled entirely from Xs and Zs."

"Fantastic." She yawned and shifted to lie in his lap. "What's my prize?"

"What do you want it to be?"

He bent over her and Norah turned her head a millisecond before their lips touched. A wave of heat burst from the pit of her stomach as his warm whisper tickled her ear.

"I want you, Norah. Tell me 'yes,' and let me take you to the bed."

Her mind screamed 'no,' but her body throbbed with a resounding plea for him. Norah arched her back pressing the apex of her neck closer to his mouth as her groin pulsed and reminded her how long it had been since anyone had touched her.

"Yes," she breathed and unleashed everything she had left to lose as Enrique grazed her earlobe with his teeth. "Now. Right here."

Norah kissed him hungrily and he wound his hands into her short hair, pulling her head gently backward to fully expose her neck as the warmth of his lips found her most sensitive spot and did not relent until she groaned and yanked at the buttons on her blouse.

"Let me." His dark eyes glinted down at her as he made quick work of what she had fumbled and peeled her shirt from her body. She caught his hand as he tossed it to the ground and moved it to the button of her jeans. He sent another chill through her as his other hand cupped her breast upward. A twinge of pain shadowed her pleasure and she pulled away to say they were sensitive, only to be immediately distracted by his pushing her jeans to the floor and pulling his polo over his head.

Norah looked up into his bare chest and closed her eyes as he produced a condom from the back pocket of his shorts and tore the wrapper open with his teeth.

"Don't think. Just enjoy," he whispered, sliding the latex up his length.

Norah pushed his boxers to the floor with his shorts. He slid into her gently, letting her body accept him little by little. When Enrique leaned fully into her, Norah snapped her eyes open at how quickly she was nearing orgasm. He thrust once and she rocked her hips upward to deepen the motion, trying and failing to breathe from her nose as he straightened her bent leg and pressed it to the side of his face keeping one hand on her hip and sending her reeling into an explosion of sheer pleasure more intense than she'd ever known and ending in the deepest sleep she had had in weeks.

Ellie

"Thank you for your time," Ellie repeated, thumbing the folder marked "Lindsay Procedures." She closed the door behind the guards, pressed the code to lock the steel frame, and leaned against its wooden exterior. The quiet of the room was an odd novelty after weeks spent as houseguest with constant interruptions from nurses. She slipped one heel off and then the other, noticing first the difference in the carpet pad and then the angle of Sherrie's picture on the wall.

"I wish you were here," she said to the canvass as she released the breath she hadn't realized she was holding. "I need you so much."

Ellie swallowed hard, trying to reconcile that the space she loved was forever changed and that no amount of mimicry would ever bring it back. *Center*, she told herself and walked to the kitchen by habit. A white bowl filled with her favorite pink lady apples sat on the island and she looked around, half expecting to see her housekeeper but knowing that she wouldn't. Ellie sat the folder by the apples and opened the refrigerator. It was almost exactly as she had left it, stocked with quinoa in mason jars and organic vitamin waters. Ellie took her phone from her jacket pocket and snapped a picture.

1 New Group Text: To SisterFriends

Thank you for this.

1 New Text: To Leila

This had to be you. Thank you.

Ellie chose a jar from the shelf and opened the crisper below where she kept all of her flatware in the interest of convenience. Spoon in hand, she traced her usual path to the balcony, trying to prepare herself for what would likely be the hardest difference to accept. She ignored her wan reflection in the glass door and slid it open onto the deck, immediately gasping at the sight. The space she had loved for so long was gone. The terracotta pots that held her palm trees had been replaced with sleek slate hexagons and there were no pops of turquoise and coral to be seen. Ellie walked to her favorite chaise lounge and sank into the lemon yellow cushion, its firmness screaming that it was new. She focused her attention on the waves breaking in the distance. The rhythmic sound calmed her nerves, but the chair made her feel like a guest in a hotel.

She stood and walked to the railing of the deck, still seeing the crime scene images of 'pray the gay away' written in pig's blood as she leaned against the freshly stained wood. The scent of orange peel wafted toward her and she noticed the braided trunk of a miniaturized tree recessed into a new planter. An iridescence behind the leaves caught her eye and she lifted the branches to reveal a pearlescent picture frame that had been clearly glued back together containing Kate's faded script. *New home. New dream. Same beautiful you.*

Ellie looked from the words to the waves, missing Pat. She lifted her phone and shot a quick panoramic photo from the edge of the deck and attached it to a text.

1 New Text: To Patrick Grayson

We're not finished in LA yet. Come here and we'll dream the rest of our story together.

Kate

You're welcome. Just remember, it doesn't have to be the same to be great.

Kate grinned at her phone, relieved that Ellie was pleased with her design. She had spent hours recreating the inside of the condo as a near perfect replicate of what it had been before, but had consciously chosen a different direction outside, where the damage was the most severe. She knew Ellie would see through a re-creation of a peace that never could be restored.

"Who are you texting, babe?" Ken leaned over her shoulder.

"Ellie."

"Is she home? I thought she was in London."

"She's home a little early and loves my design. I have worried and stressed that she wouldn't like it because it was different than the original. This job was unlike any other I have ever done. I can't put my finger on why. If she had hated it, I would have just re-created my first design, but I wanted her to love it...and to live her next chapter in it."

"I think the word you're looking for is 'investment.' You care more about it because you are invested in Ellie's happiness."

"Maybe so."

"Do you know what trumps that?"

"What?" She wiped Liam's chin and signed "more."

"You were happy doing it. I think you should consider consulting."

"I would never have the time. Not with—"

"With Liam? Where was he when you designed for Ellie? Or Leila's master bed and bath?"

"That was different. They're friends and I was doing them a favor."

"Just think about it. You're very talented and I'll support you if you want to start a little business."

"Maybe I will. I could keep it small and only take on a few projects at a time."

"I bet Cami or Wes would loan you an intern to set up a website. We could call it KL Designs. Kate Liam Designs."

"I like that," she said, imagining a Meyer lemon yellow card with platinum lettering and getting excited about her potential new venture.

Cami

Cami walked through Zac's door for what would be the last time as anything other than a friend.

"I'm sorry I missed our visit to Cameron."

"I get being stuck in a meeting, but you should have called."

"I know. I'm sorry. How was he?"

Cami sat on his sofa, careful to avoid the sunken spot in the middle that belonged to his ninety-pound lab, Hershey, who was padding in from the kitchen.

"Barely there. The nurses said he had a rough afternoon and trashed his pottery wheel during activities time. Speaking of sedation, do you want a drink?"

He walked to the bar cart nestled against the fireplace across the room and lifted a crystal decanter.

"No. I'm not staying."

He knitted his brows and dumped a finger of bourbon into a high-ball glass emblazoned with his restaurant's logo. Cami's instincts cried that it had to be now if she was ever going to break their after-hours habit. She didn't want to hurt him, but not doing so seemed as impossible as avoiding pain by pulling a Band-Aid slowly.

"Look, Zac. I wish there were an easier way to do this, but there isn't."

"Then don't."

"What?"

"Just don't." He sat beside her and Hershey claimed his spot, plopping a lazy head onto Zac's thigh.

"Zac, it's already gone on too long. It will never be right."

"It will be if you let it. You only want to end things now because what we have is creeping into what you've lost."

"That's not true." Cami closed her eyes and blurted out what she'd come to say before she lost her courage and kissed who he wasn't. "I want to end it because I don't like who I am when I'm with you."

Zac choked a little on his sip and either her words or the burn of the whiskey brought red lines to the surface of his eyes.

"Because I'm not Blane."

"No."

"Because you kiss me and fantasize about him? I'm not stupid, Cami. No one will ever be Blane. You have a man in front of you who loves you and who loved him. You would see that if you weren't so stubborn. I'm not even asking you to move on. I'm just asking you to make a place for me. Let me love you."

Her rage fogged her thoughts and she spit out the words she'd sworn she wouldn't say.

"It's not that simple! You have no idea what it's like for me being with you. Every single time I leave feeling like I've betrayed him. Like I'm sleeping with his best friend while he's gone. What's worse is I feel like the Greene family is peeking through your window rooting for us. It's like they're saying *C'mon, Cami! This will make it all okay. Then, we can stop worrying about you.*"

"And you don't see any sense in that? I'll say it again. I love you enough to be second. Let us grow. We'll move on and start a new normal together. Let me date you. Court you. I was wrong to say I wanted to love you like he would have wanted you to be loved. I should have said let me love you like your pain deserves. I don't want to mask it, I want to see it, kiss it, heal it. I want to show you my scars in return."

"I don't love you. I just miss him. Being with you is like being slapped in the face with everything I miss and ache for. I'm sorry we started this. I have to go."

Her feet pushed her to the door and her lungs finally filled when she was on the other side.

Leila

"It's fine." Leila blotted the spilled juice off of the papers she had graded and lied into the phone. It wasn't fine, she was just tired of caring. If Wes wanted to work nineteen hours a day, so be it. At least she hadn't told the girls they were having family night.

"Mommy! Mommy!" they shouted in unison as they ran into the kitchen. "Look what we found!" Clara held up a one-legged, naked Snow White doll Leila knew she had thrown away. "Can we wash her hair?"

"Yes, but not right now. Go put her in the bathtub for later."

"Yea!" They squealed and ran down the hall. Leila snapped a quick picture on her phone, wanting to remember how they ran holding hands before they outgrew it. Her stomach rumbled and she looked at the clean kitchen, not wanting to mess it up and not wanting to eat any of the food she had frozen.

"Who wants to take Mommy to dinner?" she called, smiling at the girls' enthusiastic *I do! I do!*, trailing down the hall and, in a moment of weakness, agreed they could wear their princess dresses.

1 New Text: To Kate Cell

I'm taking the girls to dinner at Zapata's. Want to join us?

Reply: From Kate Cell

Want to terrify a hostess? Ask for a table of five, two kids'
menus, and a high chair.

1 New Text: To Kate Cell

This is true. Want to join our crazy?

Reply: From Kate Cell

Liam has been really fussy this afternoon, so I am in for
the night. See you for breakfast Thursday tho.

Leila wondered if Kate really didn't want to go out, or if she just didn't
want to eat.

Ellie

"I miss you, too," Ellie said as the last bit of light faded into the sea.

"I keep expecting you to come into the room, then I have to remind myself you're back in the States."

"It feels strange to be alone in my kitchen after so many days of dodging nurses in yours."

"Don't get too used to it. I'll be leaving crumbs in your sink again before you know it. Ay! Christ, that's hot."

Ellie laughed as she heard some sort of dish land loudly on a counter.

"What are you doing?"

"Blythe and I went to a noodle shop and I am heating up leftovers. Or making a mess rather."

"I saw her at the airport. It was more than a little awkward."

"She told me as much."

"Listen, I don't know why, but it bothers me that she's there and I'm not."

It also bothers me that you knew she left my firm and didn't tell me.

"Ellie, we're no more than good friends."

"I know, but it still bothers me for some reason."

"You're cute when you're jealous."

Ellie could hear the smile in his voice.

"Would it make you feel better if I told you she was engaged?"

"She is?"

"Yes, as of one week ago. They've managed to keep it out of the papers by some act of magic. I'm to be the best man."

"I hate to say it, but that doesn't make me feel any better given her history. We both know fidelity isn't one of her strengths."

"You really are jealous. I think I'm flattered."

"Not funny."

"I promise you've nothing to worry about. Can I ring you back in a bit? I am going to eat and then go to church with my family."

"Of course." Ellie refilled her wine, thinking she hadn't had a conversation involving parents and an ex-girlfriend since her teen years.

Norah

Norah woke in pain. Her lower abdomen felt like it had been stuffed with sand. She let out a small whimper and pushed herself upright. *Breathe,* she told herself. *Just breathe. You are not having a miscarriage. You are constipated. You've eaten nothing but sodium, dairy, and pre-natal vitamins for days.*

"Are you okay?" Enrique sat up beside her and reached for her hand.

"I think so."

"Lie back. Are you contracting?"

"Ouch." Norah winced at the motion and Enrique placed one hand on her lower abdominals and one hand over her navel.

"When was your last BM? Do you want me to run and get you a soft-ener, or a smoothie?"

"No. It will pass." She winced again and began to sweat, thinking this was likely the least romantic conversation to ever take place in a ho-tel bed and wondering why she suddenly missed Matt.

"You're warm, Norah. We need to take you in. Do you want me to call someone?"

"I'm fine. I just need sleep." Norah's sweat chilled her skin and she passed a puff of gas.

"What would you want your patient to do?" Enrique said as his pager buzzed on the nightstand. "See? I'm probably going there anyway."

"Fine." Norah sat up again and forced her legs over the bed, thinking at least she would get hydrated and hoping none of her nurses moonlighted at Enrique's hospital.

Leila

"Your girls are so well-behaved. If mine had been that good, we would have gone out to eat every night!" A silver-haired patron with a smart layered bob stopped at their table on her way to the restroom.

"What do we say, girls?"

"Thank you!" they replied and continued coloring.

"I appreciate you stopping to say that. We love this special time."

"We are having a guh-wirls' night."

"Because Daddy's at work," Julia finished.

"Like always, I'm sure." The woman gave Leila a knowing look. "Good job, mom. It took me decades longer to learn that if my workaholic husband wouldn't take me out, I would take myself out on his dime."

"I think I'll start doing it more often." Leila smiled and decided to order dessert.

Cami

Cami wasn't sure if the air was actually nicer this morning or if she just felt lighter. The last two miles of her run had not been this easy in months. Another runner passed with a muscled dog trotting beside his thigh and she thought about Zac and Hershey. Did the Greenes know she had trampled on the heart of a man they considered to be their son by another mother? Were they angry? Probably. Cami crossed the street, cursing that doing the right thing was so hard. She saved her time on her Apple watch and noticed she had missed five texts. That was odd at this hour.

1 New Group Text: From Wes Oliver

I'm texting all of you because I want to do something for Leila's birthday and I need your help. If I ask her, she will say let's just go to Zapata's and I want it to be special.

1 New Text: From Ellie

We can have it in Malibu.

1 New Text: From Kate

She will love this, Wes. I'm thinking tapas and decoup-
aged pictures. We can call it 'Life of Leila.'

1 New Text: From Kate

Wait! That's totally insensitive to Pat! Forget everything
I just said!

Cami read the messages and wondered how much trouble Wes was in to
prompt him to add 'party thrower' to his resume. She had always suspected that, in far different ways from Matt and Norah, things weren't as
peachy at home as Leila made them out to be. Cami was the first to admit
she didn't understand Leila's obsession with gratitude and with finding
the good in every problem. There were no such things as good problems. Problems existed to ask questions, and could only be solved with
actions, not philosophies. She swiped the messages away and stretched
her hamstring wondering if Leila believed her own act.

Leila

"I'm not mad, Wes. I'm disappointed," Leila said into the phone, trying to find a pair of black underwear that wouldn't criss-cross the fat on her bottom into a waffle iron grid beneath her leggings. "I want to be on your radar not because I throw a fit and demand your attention, but because you crave time with me the way I do with you. The way you act on date night makes me feel like you're just checking off a box on your to-do list. Every morning, I plan the day and every morning I notice that I am planning it around you—the variable I can't control. I don't care that you miss dinner. I care that we wait. I feel like the girls and I are stuck in some sort of bizarre solar system that orbits around you and pauses based on your interest in us. Which, in that regard, seems slight at best."

"That's not fair, beautiful. I love you and the kids."

"It is fair. I know you love us and furthermore I make sure they know it when you're not here. Do you know what I would give to be you in their eyes? You throw a tiny crumb of affection at them and they eat on it for days. All I hear is Daddy did X, while I meet their every other need."

"So you're resentful?"

"That's not what I'm saying, Wes. I'm saying I paint a picture of their dad for them that I believe is true. You work harder than hard for our family. You love us. You are at work to provide opportunities for us. What I'm also saying is that it would be nice if you just *showed up*. For them, or for me, with a happy heart and saw them the way you see your job." Leila wiped away the hot tears streaming down her cheeks, mad that she had broken the first rule she ever made for herself...never cry over a man. "Something's got to give before they're too old to care where you are."

Norah

"Do you want me to call anyone before my surgery?" Enrique asked, looking at his phone.

"Do you mean Matt? I don't want to open that can of worms. "

"Or your mom? Or the friend I called once before, Laura I think it was."

"Leila," Norah said, hating his persistence and wishing he would simply acknowledge the elephant in the room. "We both know how minor this is. We both know you can't stay."

"And we both know you don't want me to."

"It's not that. I just don't want the fuss. I'm going to work as soon as I drain this bag." Norah willed the saline dripping into her veins to finish faster.

"Unless they order an enema."

"Not happening. Go to your surgery."

Enrique grinned, looked over each of his shoulders, and kissed her before he left the room.

Ellie

"It's truly hard to believe the progress he's made." Ellie reached across her desk and took her stack of mail from the young man. "You're very blessed, Ms. Lindsay. Have yourself a good day now."

"Thank you. We are looking forward to moving on."

She flipped through the event invitations addressed to her and Pat, flicking each one into the bin, until a cardboard Fed-Ex mailer caught her finger with its weight. Ellie sat the rest of the correspondence to the side and pulled its perforated tabs apart. The cards Pat had tied to her stairs tumbled into her lap and her hands trembled as she picked up the letter that followed them.

> *Dear Ellison,*
>
> *I am <u>not</u> sorry for taking these. I picked them up as trash and just when I was about to drop them in the recycling bin, I saw the handwriting. These notes were not written to the woman I spent three years working for. That woman barely knew my name and kept me pinned under Jess. I'll work for one of you again, but it won't be you. That said, I'm not a monster. Here are your promises. Consider them a thank you for my raise.*
>
> *— Stacie*

The stationary was embossed with Jess Franklin Public Relations, LLC. Ellie fingered the raised font and picked up Pat's cards, more certain than ever that all of her stories were destined to end in betrayal.

Kate

No. No. No. No. It was too soon. Kate stared at the pregnancy tests in front of her, calculating that Liam would be a toddler when his sibling was born and dreading hearing the words *Irish twins* come out of her mother's mouth.

Leila

I New Text: From Kate Cell

I took the first one because I am two days late. The next
three were supposed to tell me it was lying.

*L*eila read the text, equally excited and anxious for her friend,
and tried to find the right words to tell Kate that she would be
okay.

Reply: To Kate Cell

Wow! I have so much to say and no time to type it. You
can do this. There are tons of advantages to having children so close in age. I often think about that when I am
repeating all of the "threenager" things that tried my
patience the first time around with Clara. Think of it
as a two for one special in that they will both learn their
expectations and boundaries together.

Leila pressed send on her message, typed a quick check-in with Torri to make sure the girls were behaving, and double-checked that she had locked her car before walking toward the patched chain link fence surrounding the trailer that had been her childhood home.

"So you didn't bring your kids?" Tanya stood smoking on the porch.

"Not this time," Leila said unhooking the horseshoe-shaped latch on the fence and trying hard not to engage Tanya.

"This time. *Humph.*" She rolled her eyes and Leila debated turning back to her car. "You say that like this is something you do every day. You ain't been here in years."

"I wonder why." Leila meant to say it in her head, but the words hit her ears and she regretted actually speaking them. There was no nostalgia for her here, only regrets, confusion, and a dread of reliving the memories she had run from.

"Well, it ain't because of me. That's all on you." Tanya flicked her finished cigarette butt into the yard as Leila climbed the rickety, ash-laden, steps to the door, envying what going home must feel like to normal people.

Norah

"It's better that you came in. Dr. Merrit would have made you if your husband hadn't." Jillian finished saying as Norah slipped on her gloves.

"She's right," Norah smiled.

She explained the exam she was about to perform, ignoring the husband's discomfort. Jillian asked if they had chosen a name and made the usual small talk. Norah's suspicions were correct and her patient was at least a week away from delivery. She assuaged her fears that she had overreacted, talked about how intense pre-term contractions, called Braxton-Hicks, could be, and peppered in an anecdote about how one of her patients had had them so frequently that 'Braxton' started to have a ring to it and would become her baby's middle name. She left the room with a hug that reaffirmed how her care made her a part of these families long after delivery.

Ellie

*I*t's not true. He wouldn't. Would he? Ellie's mind raced around the pictures filling her screen, certain her office walls were closer together than they had been thirty seconds ago.

"Ms. Lindsay?"

"It can wait," she snapped as Pat's name lit up her phone.

The assistant backed cautiously out of the door.

"Hello?"

"Ellie, you have to let me explain."

"Do you have time or are you still busy breaking the Internet?" Ellie hissed into the fear on the other end of the line.

"It's not what it looks like."

"Then what is it, Pat? All I see is you and your ex-girlfriend having a *Lady and the Tramp* moment over some noodles."

"It's painted that way. I'll give you that much, but it's simply untrue. I'm asking for your trust here Ellie."

"Do you have any idea how foolish this makes me look?" Ellie's temples throbbed in unison with her tapping foot.

"I know. And I'm sorry. So terribly sorry. Tell me you believe me."

Ellie stared at the pictures of Blythe wiping a sauce streaked noodle remnant from his chin and eating a snow pea from his chopsticks. Her gut told her it was innocent, but she didn't trust it.

"Is there anything else I need to know?"

"Of course not."

He sounded hurt and she could hear the tap of his cane on the ground as he paced.

"What you're seeing is old friends sharing a meal. She went back to her hotel straight after to get ready for a nightclub opening and I went to church with my family."

Ellie flipped through Blythe's Instagram and compared the time stamps on the photos. Pat apologized again and she met his words with an icy acceptance, staring at the cards on her desk, knowing how quickly flirtation with Mr. Grayson could spiral.

"Look, Ellie. This is me groveling. I should have been more careful. Her bodyguard scouted it before we went in and there were two, maybe three people there. Each of them was elderly and uninterested. I realize how coquettish it all looks, but it didn't feel that way."

Ellie's team waited impatiently beyond her glass walls and she shuffled the cards and letter into her top desk drawer. The embossed name of Jess's new firm caught the light and sent her instincts haywire.

"It's Jess," she whispered into the phone. "She must have tipped off a photographer. Every magazine in the UK and the US will print this, she will spin Blythe out of it, and her brand will grow. It's as brilliant as it is deceptive."

"And every last story will question my commitment to you."

"Naturally." Ellie's anger rose again as her head of social media joined the fray outside. "My team is on the verge of breaking down my door. I need to go."

"I'm sorr—"

"I know."

She waved the team in and pointed toward the conference table.

"Goodbye."

Cami

"**S**o you've met Pat Grayson, Clark?" Dean swung his racquet hard and she lunged to return the serve.

"Don't need to. It's obvious that he's using her." Cami wiped the sweat from her forehead with the tail of her shirt, impressed again by how much of a workout thirty minutes of racquetball was.

"You really think so? I get a 'good guy' vibe from him, but what do I know?" He jetted backward and sent the ball spinning toward the ceiling.

"I have no doubt he can deliver a line, but trust me when I say this whole situation is bizarre for Ellie."

"Ellie? It's strange to hear Ellison Lindsay referred to so casually. You must be very good friends." Dean's voice echoed against the wall as he overshot and missed the ball.

"We are," Cami said, trying to estimate how mad Ellie still was about the Marcus article and realizing how much she had missed her while she was gone. "And now that Mr. Hollywood is out of the picture, things will be back to normal."

"Out of the picture? Doesn't look that way online. The post I saw said Blythe Barrett was there specifically because Ellison Lindsay had to be back in LA and wanted Pat to have company."

THWACK!

"There's no way Ellie is that stu—" Cami retorted, charging the ball, but raising her racquet a millisecond too late to block it.

A searing pain sent her reeling backwards as the rubber became one with her cheekbone and landed her on her haunches. She cupped her bleeding upper lip in her hands, feeling like her face had exploded. Dean's shoulder was beneath her in an instant, lifting her to her feet like she was weightless. She pushed him off at first, mumbling that she was fine, but only seeing stars and sinking back to the dusty floor.

"C'mon, Clark."

He lifted her again and carried her to a teak bench against the wall. She protested that she was fine, but his answer was a clean towel.

"Head back while I get some ice."

Cami was too stunned to argue more and sat there until he returned with the mercifully cold ice pack.

"So, maybe golf next time?" He angled his arm under her head and let the cool numb her already bruising cheek.

"No hustle points in golf," she laughed painfully and took in the musky smell of him for the first time.

Ellie

"**Y**ou know better than anyone how this looks," she said to Blythe's apology.

"I'm so sorry. Pat is really concerned and my fiancée is furious. He knows I'm here, with, um, Pat, but, well, he didn't realize we would be alone. I told him you were here, too. Can't I just fix it by flying home tomorrow and tweeting about getting back to the love of my life?"

"Did Jess tell you to do that?"

"No. She said to let the pictures with Pat be distractors until I want to announce my engagement."

"The pictures will definitely do that, for as long as social media gives them life, but what do you want? If you want to help Pat and dodge the adulterer rep that's following you, then you need to tell the truth. If I were still in London, I would have been the third wheel in the noodle house and this would all be irrelevant."

"Jess won't like it, but I'll post as soon as I'm in the air. Do you think that will make it hell when I land?"

"If there's one thing I know about Jess," Ellie punched the button to signal her new assistant, "it's that she knows how to have a plane met. If I were you, I would ask my publicist."

Leila

1 New Group Text: From Ellie Cell

Who can meet for dinner tonight? I miss you guys and apparently need to prove my happiness to the Internet.

"Do you ever put that thing down?" Tanya pointed at the phone in Leila's hand and handed Darla a can of snuff. "Now don't go lookin' at me like I lit a cigarette," Darla said in Leila's direction. "It ain't the same and it ain't gonna catch my tank on fire."

"It's a bad habit. I shouldn't be so attached to it." Leila tucked her phone into her purse.

"We all got our addictions, don't we? Anyway, you look really pretty today, Leigh Anne."

"Thank you. I came straight from work."

"Well, we know it wasn't for us!" Tanya spit as she tied her orange bakery apron around her waist. "She wears gym clothes to therapy."

Leila squirmed. "Those are my days off."

"My day off is spelled l-a-u-n-d-r-y. There's so much of it that I think there's people living here wearin' our clothes we ain't met yet."

"I know you work hard, Tanya, and have a lot of responsibilities. No argument here. Can I help with the laundry? I could take some and bring it back with me to therapy or here on Saturd—"

"How many clothes you think we got each? Listen to her, Mamma. She thinks we can make do for a week without a Laundromat stop. I'll bring home milk and bologna, Daddy. Text me if you think of anything else."

"I actually brought you guys some groceries. Mom said things have been extra tight with the added gas you're using to get to her appointments."

"You can take them back home with you, too," Ronnie spoke for the first time. "We don't need no charity from you."

"Just stop it, both of you," Darla said through the onset of a coughing fit. "That was nice of you, Leigh Anne."

"I want to help. I just don't know how. Tell me what you need."

"I'd like to get to know my granddaughters. I want you to start bringing them here."

Why here? Leila screamed silently as Ronnie lit another cigarette and blew his smoke in her direction.

Cami

"It's really nothing. Like I told Kate, I am learning to play racquetball and misjudged the ball. What about you? You smell like a bar. Where in the hell have you been?"

"Thanks. I'm glad you're okay," Leila deadpanned as she turned her attention to the menu.

Cami knew she had said something wrong when Kate rolled her eyes, but the words to make it better escaped her. They sat in silence until Norah bustled into Zapata's and headed to their table with one of her standard reasons for being late.

"Anyway, I got here as quickly as I could."

Norah slipped into the chair next to her, and Cami noticed her pale blue scrubs were getting tighter on her small frame. She looked puffier and somehow more drawn than Kate or Leila had during this part of their pregnancies.

"Whoa. What happened to your face, Cami? Are you okay? Cami? Are you listening?"

"Sorry. This would be the result of a racquetball fail. I took it up as a stress reliever and, evidently, am out of my league."

"Ouch. You're lucky you didn't break any teeth."

"Maybe I'll buy a lottery ticket."

"I'm surprised we all beat Ellie here. She must be slammed on her first day back," Leila said, passing Norah the carafe of mineral water.

"Thanks." Norah poured it into the highball glass in front of her and added a packet of orange flavored fiber powder. "I needed this."

"I remember those days," Leila commiserated.

Cami watched Kate squirm uncomfortably, wondering if she was going to stay lost in space all night.

"Oh. Fiber and liquids. I get it now. You're constipated."

"Yes, Cami. Enough so that I woke in pain and Enrique took me with him to the hospital. Today was my day surgery morning and going in threw everything hours behind schedule."

"Why not go to your own hospital?"

"Gossip."

"Ah. Speaking of which, has everyone seen the pictures of Mr. Hollywood chowing down with his ex-girlfriend?"

"What?" Leila all but shrieked and opened Facebook at warp speed. "Did Ellie have a heart attack? Has anyone checked on her?"

"She probably saw it before we did."

"We're about to find out. She's here."

They all turned their heads to see Ellie crossing the room looking impeccable in a crisp cream shift dress with gold bangles clinking down her arm.

"She looks amazing," Kate said.

"She looks happy," Leila added.

"She's acting."

Cami's blunt observation silenced the table.

Ellie

"**I**'ve missed you so much!"

Leila was the first to hug her and Ellie disregarded the tears welling in her eyes. Leila always almost cried when she was happy.

"I've missed you, too," Ellie said as Leila flushed and sat back down.

She embraced them all in turn, finally feeling like she was home. Something was different about Norah, but she couldn't place it. Kate looked like she was trying to swallow something sour. Cami was watching them all as critically as she always did after any major change. Ellie took the empty chair beside Kate, poured water from the carafe Leila handed her, and pushed the breadbasket toward Cami in the interest of losing the weight she had gained in London.

"Hulllloooo Squad Lindsay! I'll be taking care of your every single need tonight!" A waiter who could easily have stepped off of the pages of *GQ* spun his tray on his forefinger while another sat champagne flutes in front of each of them. "No squad is complete without a little fizz. But, before you thank me, I should tell you that Ms. Lindsay—can I call you Ellie?—Not there yet?—Okay—Ms. Lindsay requested it with the reservation. She done got you the Dom!"

Norah raised her hand to stop him when he reached for her flute. "None for me."

"So sad. More for the rest of you!" The waiter winked and filled Cami's glass. "You first, because you look like the most likely to hit me."

"I took a racquetball to the face, but I like the way you think." Cami passed her glass to Kate, knowing champagne was her favorite.

"Ah! And you get the most, my lovely." He expertly filled Ellie's flute so the bubbles stopped neatly at the brim. "Shhh! I have a secret plan to ply Ms. Lindsay with bubbly and become her favorite waiter so she'll request me when the gaaaaawww-jus Mr. Grayson comes to town." He flipped his towel over his shoulder and posed with one hand on his jutted hip. "Who loves you? Rupert does."

Ellie laughed and lifted her glass. "To Rupert!"

"Thanks, doll! I'll be right back with the crab dip."

"So much for getting back on track after my London gym hiatus." Ellie sipped her champagne and basked at how nice it was to be reunited with her sister-friends.

"I think you look great," Kate spoke to her for the first time.

"Are you all right?" Cami asked from the other side of the table with a rare perceptiveness that told Ellie she must sense something urgent in Kate.

"Yes and no. I'm pregnant again." Kate went white and Cami's eyes threatened to bulge out of her head.

"So soon?" Cami blurted as Leila quietly patted Kate's hand.

"Well, it wasn't planned. That's all I want to say about it right now."

"But you're okay?"

"Yes, Cami. I promise."

"Okay. Remind me not to drink after any of you!" Cami whistled. "That's almost fifty percent of us!"

"Wait? What? Who else?" Ellie looked around the table, her eyes settling on Leila.

"Oh, God, no! Not me!" Leila shook her head still holding Kate's hand. "I mean it's great for Kate and Norah, but—"

"Norah? What? Norah!" Ellie said more critically than she intended then attempted to soften her shock with a breezy, "Congratulations are in order, right?"

"It was a surprise to say the least," Norah bristled. "But I'm happy about it. My life may be a mess, but this part makes me want to keep putting one foot in front of the other until I figure the rest out."

"To babies!" Leila raised her champagne. "And new beginnings."

They clinked their glasses and Ellie snapped a picture on her phone.

"I won't post it until later. I just wanted to remember the moment. "It's been hard being away." She closed her camera and felt the mood at the table shift. "Really hard and I have no idea where I go from here. I'm sure you've seen the noodle house pictures by now."

"I don't trust him," Cami said.

"You don't know him," Ellie snipped.

"But I do have eyes."

"As do I. Visit any nightclubs with your personal trainer lately? Facts and photos aren't always the same thing."

Ellie stared coldly at Cami for a moment, then looked into each of their faces separately. Norah was gathering facts. Leila was on love's side. Kate was hungry to believe in him.

"I don't expect any of you to understand why I trust him when I barely know myself. That said, Ca-Noodle-Gate isn't the only bombshell I'm processing. He doesn't want to come back to the US permanently. He's been offered a role in the West End playing Mr. Darcy opposite of Blythe Barrett in a modern day adaptation of *Pride and Prejudice*."

"He would be a perfect Darcy!"

Kate's mood swing to fan girl made Ellie smile.

"He really would, but as much as I hate the idea of a long-distance, much less intercontinental, relationship, I know he really would be happier there. He keeps saying he isn't as tempted by the role as by the fact that he feels safer in London."

"And his family is there. That has to be a factor," Leila added.

"Which brings us to what feels like the five hundredth obstacle in our way—Mathilda Grayson. His mother wants him home and has a lot of influence over him. Possibly more than I do."

"I don't get it." Cami buttered another piece of bread. "Your boyfriend is snuggling up to his old flame an ocean away and his mother is your biggest concern?"

"No, Cami. Blythe is engaged. It's just not public knowledge yet. *Destiny* gave them a bond I'll never understand, but I get the feeling something else is going on here. Jess quit to start her own firm and Blythe left with her. She has a lot to gain by convincing him to agree to play Darcy, and a lot to lose by being rebranded as 'the other woman' like she was after she cheated on him when they were a couple."

"The dreaded other woman," Norah commented, but didn't seem offended.

"What are you telling us, Ellie? Are you moving to England? What about the firm? What about your life? It's here."

"I don't know, Cami. I'm telling you that I don't know. Everything is different now. I want him to be safe and I want him with me."

"That's what real love does," Leila said. "It changes your priorities. You'll find a new stride and the right choice will be clear soon. I know so."

Ellie looked into Leila's eyes, not knowing how she seemed so convincing.

Cami

"And then there were two." Ellie signed her tab, watching Norah hug Leila and Kate goodbye just before the door. "You missed a lot more than what was said tonight," Cami sighed and scrutinized her bill to make sure they hadn't been charged for Kate's split plate.

"I guessed as much. How are you and Zac?"

"There is no 'me and Zac.' It's over. It wasn't mutual, but it's over."

Cami felt her brows knit as Ellie tried to act surprised.

"That must have been hard."

"He kept looking at me like I had just kicked his dog. I know he's hurting because he hasn't texted me. He used to ping me five times a day just to say hello or to send me a meme he thought I would like. I don't know which one is worse—the silence or the attention."

"It sounds like you miss him."

"Not in that way. I miss the friend I had before I crossed a line and screwed everything up."

"I get that. I crossed a line and now it's like I'm not even myself anymore. I can't even look in the mirror without thinking about Pat. I miss everything about him."

"Damn. I was banking on you and Mr. Hollywood being a fling."
Cami laughed, then immediately regretted the words when Ellie looked
down at the table.

"I know it doesn't make sense. All I can say is that, from the very
beginning, two days with him felt like six months. Then, beside his bed
after the surgeries, and when we went back to London for cryotherapy,
every hour together felt like we grew into something more. It's as if our
commitment went through a trial by fire and survived."

"Is that why those pictures don't bother you?"

"Oh, they *bother* me. *Bother* might be the understatement of the year.
They're innocent, but there's a truth there."

"I don't get it. He's not cheating on you, but he could?"

"More like he has nightmares and she is the one he calls for."

"Wow."

Cami wished she had the right words to tell Ellie she was about to
have her heart handed to her on a star-shaped platter.

Leila

"Their entire relationship has been out of character for Ellie," Leila said, taking her earrings out and putting them on the counter as Wes spooned another bite of cereal into his mouth. "She trusts him in a way that makes me know it's right. I think that's why she sent him to her house in the first place when the picture of him on the ski slope with Scarlett James broke."

"That's a good point, beautiful. Here's hoping she's not just the latest ingénue in his pattern."

"*Ellie the ingénue.* That's cute." Leila laughed and popped a chamomile tea pod into the Keurig. "There should have been leftover chicken and sweet potatoes from the kids' dinner unless Torri ate more than usual."

"There were." He yawned. "I was just in the mood for something I could eat dead on my feet before I crash."

"Long day?" She added an ice cube to her steaming mug and filled another glass with water for Wes, who had likely had nothing to drink since lunch.

"I'm starting to wonder if there's any other kind. This quarter seems to be our worst yet. I promise I am not there because I don't want to be here."

"I know."

"You're looking at me like I'm letting you down. Is it because I didn't eat what you cooked for the girls? Torri was just getting them to bed when I got here, so I let her leave early and I read them stories."

"That's great, Wes. I'm glad you got that time with them."

She knew her voice sounded removed and she quieted her urge to snap that getting anything *but* cereal on the table every night required her pre-planning and prepping on Sunday. Maybe she should just quit cooking and call it good.

"I know it's not enough. I'm trying. I really am."

"I know, Wes. I just miss you. I miss us. I can't even remember the last time we spent any real time together. Worse than that, I feel like I am starting a new chapter in my life that you're completely unvested in."

"Do you mean seeing the therapist with your mom? I don't know what you want from me there."

"No, Wes. I did not mean my mom. And, honestly, would it matter if I did? Would you be able to be with me after those awful therapy sessions if I asked?"

He looked scared she would actually ask him to and that further fueled her indignity.

"Don't worry, I won't ask. I meant that I feel like my returning to teaching is a new chapter for me and you are almost wholly unaware because, like almost everything else, it happens while you're gone."

"Then tell me what you want. How do I know I'm screwing up if you act like everything's fine? How is that fair?"

"I didn't say you were screwing up. Those are your words. I said I am tired of feeling like the girls and I are 'out of sight, out of mind' in ninety percent of your day. You say to tell you what I want, then balk at the idea of having to give it. How is *that* fair? What if I asked you to be here to help with the girls on the nights I record lectures so I could start them after dinner, before they go to bed? Can you commit to that? For me? So I can finish before midnight and we can actually spend time together? My guess is 'no' given the look on your face and the fact that the last thing you committed to was being home on Tuesdays and Thursdays for dinner. That hasn't happened in weeks."

"So you're keeping count?"

"I'm not. But, you will look up two more hectic quarters from now and the girls will be too old not to notice. The days of them being thrilled that Daddy is home will be vapors before you know it."

"Why do you act like they will be driving tomorrow?"

"Because they will be. For all intents and purposes, Wes, they will be and you will have missed almost everything. I've said a million times that the days are long and the years are short."

"Look, Leila, it's late. We're both tired. Let's leave this at 'I will do better, for you and for them, and keep myself accountable.'"

"Okay." She sipped the hot liquid in her mug to stave off the shudder that crept up her back and made her skin prickle into bumps every time they argued. "I'm sorry for getting emotional. You know it's not lost on me that I can be with the girls and only teach part time because of your salary. I know you love what you do and I'm not asking you to change that. I'm just trying to make sure the rest of your life isn't passing you by. When was the last time you enjoyed a dinner that didn't come out of a box with a cartoon tiger on the front."

"Tonight." He grinned and slanted the bowl in her direction before pouring the rainbow-tinted milk down the drain. "This dinner was brought to you by a modern Stone Age family."

"Ha. Add a dinosaur vitamin and at least you're getting your recommended daily allowance of nostalgia." Leila shook her head at him and mirrored his yawn. "Let's go to bed. We can round out your healthy choices with some cardio."

Ellie

Ellie thanked her driver and congratulated him on the birth of his third son as well as on his fifth anniversary with her company, making a note to send a loyalty bonus his way. Her heels clicked over the pavers leading to the garage entry and for the smallest moment she gave into the normalcy of routine and forgot that everything in her world had changed. She entered her code and watched the newly installed fingerprint recognition pad glow green as it confirmed her identity and released the deadbolts.

The air in the mudroom was chilled and still held the acrid scent of fresh paint. She climbed the three steps to the living room entry by muscle memory, shedding her blazer and opening the door before leaning on the wall to remove one shoe and then the other. Ellie traced her usual path to the kitchen, frowning at the mason jar of salad she had left beside the sink and walking to the refrigerator out of habit. She took a bottle of vitamin water from the shelf as her phone buzzed with an email notification. Ellie skimmed the subject line and continued what had once been her nightly decompression ritual. She flipped one light on and then another, feeling gloriously alone and intensely lonely all at the same time. The salty air rushed into the room as she slid the patio door open and stepped out into the space that had always been her sanctuary.

The moon hung orange and heavy in the sky, reflecting in flickering beams upon the waves.

Ellie wiggled into the cushion of her new chair and shut her eyes, determined not to let tomorrow's questions dominate her thoughts. She focused on the rhythm of the crashing water and rolled her neck from side to side in a futile attempt to coerce her muscles to release their knots. The conversations of the evening echoed in her ears and she wavered between being warmed by Leila's enthusiasm and warned by Cami's skepticism.

"How's this for full circle."

"AHHHHH!" Startled by the male voice, she lunged into the top of a sit-up. Her hand found her heart as her eyes blinked Pat's silhouette into recognition.

"Pat! What? How?"

She clutched her pounding chest and followed her legs off of the side of her chair. He stood beside the open patio door, backlit by the living room lights, grinning at her. Ellie rushed to him as happy as she was confused.

"Why?" was all she managed over her leaping heart and reached up to touch the stubble on his cheek.

"It would seem I had an open-ended ticket and an invitation." He ran his hand through his hair, shaking slightly on his cane.

"Pat, I, I don't know what to say."

She threw her arms around his neck and noticed the security guards standing a few feet behind him for the first time. Reality pierced her enthusiasm and she released him, standing straighter.

"We were following procedure, Ms. Lindsay. Mr. Grayson asked to announce his own presence and is on your independent entry list."

"Of course." She nodded. "And I appreciate your diligence."

"We'll show ourselves out."

"Thank you," Pat said, never taking his eyes from hers.

"Looks like it's my turn to sweep you off of your feet, Mr. Grayson."

Ellie put her hand over his on the handle of the cane, listening for the sound of the bolt as the guards made their exit.

Leila

Regardless of his flaws, or of theirs as a couple, she still loved being in Wes's arms now as much as she had the first time they had made love.

A long married colleague had once told her that if she dropped a penny into a jar for every time they made love during their first year of marriage, and took one out for every time they made love in the years following, she would never empty the first jar. Leila knew that was true for many couples and was proud that instead of stagnating after more than a decade and two children together they still enjoyed each other several times a week. They worked each other's bodies like combination locks, knowing exactly how many touches here, then there, and what pressures in what spots would send the other seizing.

Leila hooked her leg around his waist the way she always did and waited for the sensation beginning inside of her to deepen and swallow her whole as he slowed his pace and followed her over the edge.

Ellie

"I don't know how you managed to pull this off, but I'm grateful that you did."

Ellie laid her head on Pat's shoulder and caressed the soft denim on his inner thigh.

"My life seems full of questions right now, many of which I can't answer. This one was easy. As soon as you left, I felt like half of me went with you. I started scheming to arrive early the minute I saw your text with the photo of the balcony. The medical clearance was much easier than securing the plane."

"You mean Blythe wasn't good company?" she laughed.

He went rigid beneath her. "Please don't be stuck on that, Ellie. She's always going to be a part of my life. And of our lives for that matter, assuming you let me stay in yours."

"I know," Ellie wanted to honor how much the two of them had been through together on their rise to instant fame, but their bond bothered her.

"She's an important part of my circle, Ellie. Whereas yours is made up of girlfriends, mine is Blythe, two true mates, and my family. Try to think of her as I do, like a sister. That's the only way I see her now."

"I'll try, Pat, but it's not that simple. You loved her once. I recall you were committed enough that you told Oprah you bought the ranch in Montana to raise your children together in the open air."

"I did. When I bought the ranch, I believed Blythe and I would be forever. We may have found our road back to friendship, but that's all. Trust is everything to me and she ceased being a part of that dream when she was unfaithful. I kept the ranch for myself, for the family I still hope to have one day. For *this*." He held her closer and tilted her chin up to kiss her lips. "I prayed I would find it again and I believe that I have."

Ellie looked away from his cobalt eyes as he said the words, knowing she should remind him now that even if she could bring healthy, cancer-free, children into the world, she didn't want to.

"What's wrong, love? Is it that you think I want to move us to Montana? I don't. It's just something stored away for the future."

"Another question you can't answer."

"Neither can you. Right now, it's just a vacation home."

"I don't own any long underwear."

Ellie kissed him to exit the conversation and table the looming discussion of motherhood for another day. Tonight, they were home, they were safe, and they were together.

Norah

"My wife doesn't even know what kind of soup I like. I would rather drink from a toilet bowl than eat miso."

"Why doesn't it matter to you that I made the effort to change into real clothes before we met, and prioritized our dinner so I would be on time? Why is the fact that I couldn't guess which soup you would prefer more important than anything else I *did* do? Why didn't you just set it aside, or order something else?"

"Did you feel like Norah ordered something you wouldn't like on purpose?" the therapist asked.

"My point is what kind of wife can't order off of a menu for her husband? I sat down and saw those disgusting cubes of tofu and realized she doesn't know me at all."

"*Kind* of wife? Are you serious, Matt?" Norah fumed.

"Let's take a second to calm down. We are here to communicate, not to argue."

"Agreed." Norah rubbed her forehead. "This is clearly about more than soup. I feel like nothing I ever do will be good enough for Matt. In this case, if it hadn't been the wrong soup, it would have been something equally trivial. He always lets one detail gone wrong ruin everything."

"We aren't here to blame. We are here to become better partners." Dr. Crinson scribbled a note on her tablet.

"I see what I need in our friends' marriages, and in my parents' forty years together, and I saw it in the brand-new couple beside us at that hibachi table. It's Norah who needs to learn how to be a partner."

"What is it that you need, Matt?" The therapist poised her pen to make another note.

"To come first."

The bitter ultimatum in those three little words dimmed the *I love yous* of the young Matt who had filled her travel mug with coffee every morning and stopped by the hospital on his lunch hour just to see her. That man had wanted to be her equal, not be worshipped by her.

"I regret marrying a woman who had no idea how to be a wife and mother."

"He's right." Norah's hand went instinctively to her stomach. "I don't know how to be his wife. I was a doctor pursuing this specialty when we met. I had dreams that weren't his mother's and aren't his sister's. He changed the rules when his career didn't pan out like he thought it would. Until then, my success was our success. He doesn't see it, but my schedule is fifty percent calmer now than it was in our early days."

"That might be marginally true, but what's wrong with wanting you home when I am home, or wanting you to cook a meal more than twice a year?"

"Here we go again. He doesn't want me to cook for him. He wants his ego fed. What he wants is the $60.00 steak and lobster for lunch and a new suit. He just doesn't want his wife to pay for it."

"I thought we weren't here to argue." Matt's snide glare snapped what little resolve she had left and her truth spilled out of her lips.

"He misses what we never were and I miss the man I married. That man wouldn't even recognize this one."

Norah's pager sounded, giving her the last reason she needed to leave.

Cami

"I'm sorry if you felt any pressure at all from us. Selfishly, I was thrilled when Zac said he planned to ask you to date. He's like a son to us just as you are like a daughter."

"It sounds incestuous when you put it that way." Cami pressed 'send' on the email she was simultaneously typing.

"It does, doesn't it?" Carolyn Greene acknowledged and Cami could hear the smile in her voice. "I want you to know it was never our intention to push you two together. I *do* think he's a good match for you, but nothing is more important to us than your happiness."

"I appreciate that." Cami swiveled her chair so that her back was to the door and away from the curse word laden argument escalating in the conference room. "Although, my cynical side thinks that ship has sailed."

"I know it feels that way." Carolyn paused. "But it won't when you let him go. He loved you more than anything and would want you to be happy. I have the same hole in my heart for him that you do, but life is so short. Enjoy it for those who can't."

"I know you're right, but," Cami swiveled her chair back around to see Dean standing in her doorway holding a hockey mask and a clumsily wrapped gift shaped like a racquet.

Kate

Kate scooped up the pile of sketches for her business card and wadded them into a ball. With a new baby, there wouldn't be time to start a hobby, much less a business, regardless of how confidant Ken was that she could do it all.

"You'll have ten months to get it off the ground before he or she arrives. This is good news, Kate," he had said as she cried, feeling like the most unfit mother on the planet for not wanting her pregnancy.

"Liam will have a sibling to love," he had gone on as she stewed silently that her body and her birth control had betrayed her. She knew she should go to a meeting, or make herself breakfast, but today she didn't want help; today she wanted to feel better.

Ellie

Ellie sat at the head of the conference table listening to her senior publicists debate the best approach to brand a Fortune 500 client who had clearly violated his parole as a 'reformed' dog fighter. Her heart said the photographs of him cheering a dogfight should end his career, but her pocketbook disagreed. She opened her calendar app and ticked off the meetings she had left until the one that mattered most.

Norah

Norah put another dollar in the vending machine and waited for the fifth Heath bar to drop.

"Honey, are you going to do everything we tell our patients not to do?" Jillian's cheery voice filled the break room and Norah turned around to see her ruddy cheeks and magenta scrubs.

"But nothing else tastes good with my whiskey," Norah whined sarcastically.

"Have you tried sushi? The higher the mercury rating, the better." Jillian squeezed her shoulder. "Can I bum one from you? I owe an admin a thank you."

"Sure. They really aren't for me. Kelsey is going to make some sort of candy bouquet for my friend's birthday party tonight."

"Likely story."

She pocketed the candy bar and bustled off toward the restroom.

Leila

C lara chattered on about making hand turkeys and hollowing out a pumpkin during "messy art" as the colorful boutiques boasting smoothies and artisan collectables faded mile by mile into blocks of gritty gas stations shouting about lottery tickets and cigarette prices. Leila's fingers tightened around the wheel and she pressed the lock button a third time as a red light stopped them under a bridge next to a homeless man screaming about the Apocalypse. With the counselor's help, she had been able to convince her mother to meet her and the girls at a Burger King near the trailer park.

"And today is about to get extra exciting, Julia! We are going to meet a grandmother! Did you know we had another one?"

"Do you mean like in the storybooks? Is she going to have a wand?"

"That's a *god*mother. Like Aunt Norah."

"That's right, girls." Leila said over the drone of the GPS. "We're going to have a special snack with Mommy's mommy."

The car beside them backfired and Leila jumped in her seat, praying this would go well.

Cami

"**Y**ou didn't have to do this."

Cami lifted the racquet from its clumsy wrapping.

"Call it an apology and a tax write-off." Dean sat and fidgeted with a file folder on the edge of her desk. "I'm going to play at 7:00 if you'd like to join."

"I can't tonight."

"Hot date?"

"No, a surprise birthday party. I hate surprises, and parties for that matter, but my friend's husband convinced us to plan one."

"Oh?" He looked at her expectantly. "I had plans too, but they fell through."

"That's too bad."

Cami laid the racquet on her desk and grabbed her briefcase to leave for the day.

Ellie

"**S**hould I be nervous?" Pat asked, pulling at the perfect knot in his tie until it was crooked. "They must be thinking we are insane and I truly want them to like me."

"They will love you." Ellie dusted a bit of imaginary lint off of his shoulders and turned him to face her.

"Be honest with me."

"Okay, Cami probably won't, but she's always slow to warm up to new people and is fiercely protective of us all."

"Lovely." He frowned and flattened the crisp corners of his dress shirt. "Should I change? How formal is this gathering?"

"Trust me. They will love you because I do."

"Are you sure?"

"Yes." The relief on his face stirred her need for honesty. "Cami aside."

"To meeting the family."

He raised an invisible glass and Ellie kissed him as cheers.

Leila

"It wasn't great and it wasn't bad. The girls were really excited about playing on a new playground. I didn't realize they had never seen a metal slide before."

"I guess they wouldn't have." Wes slipped into the lane furthest from the Zapata's exit.

"I wish things could be different for them and, honestly, for myself. I wish I could erase my mom's choices and give her a better life."

"I'm sorry, beautiful."

His phone dinged with an onslaught of emails and she picked it up to read the subject lines aloud to him before could ask. His shoulders crept closer to his ears with each message she read. He missed the exit to Zapata's, brushing it off with a distracted response that there was a quicker way to get there a few miles ahead. Then he told her which emails to flag as important and which to ignore.

Kate

"**L**eave it to us to forget food. This is what happens when Leila doesn't plan things," Kate laughed from the top of the stairs. "True, but we know she'd be happy with a lot less. She will just care that we're here." Cami took their delivery and handed the security guard fifty dollars to give to the Order Up driver he had refused entry at the gate.

"And that there's wine."

Kate leaned over the bannister to fasten the 'Happy Birthday' banner she had made from re-purposed chalkboard tablets and burlap bows with twine.

"Can we be of help?"

The British voice startled her and she turned to see Lucas Lucien working his way down to the landing. For a moment, despite being balanced on the ball of one foot and bent at a right angle over Ellie's stairs, she was oblivious to anything other than his crystal smile.

"Kate, this is Patrick Grayson," Ellie said, guiding him by his elbow with her usual calm.

"Oh, *I know*," Kate blurted, dropping one of the tablets to the floor below. It narrowly missed Ken's head and landed with a thud.

"She's a huge fan!" Ken called, grinning up at her as she turned pink. "I must have watched every one of the *Destiny* movies at least fifty times with her when we were dating." He scooped the fallen tablet from the floor and took the stairs two at a time to bring it back to her. "I'm Ken Stone. It's nice to meet you."

"Now that's a celeb name if I have ever heard one." Pat took his hand from his cane and pumped Ken's offered palm.

"The pleasure is mine. Good to have you home, Ellie," Ken gave her a warm hug.

Kate unplanted her feet and tried to think of something to say that wouldn't make her sound like *Will & Grace*'s Jack meeting Cher.

"These slates are quite lovely. You've definitely put the bits of paper I scrawled on to shame."

Kate responded in her head, then lost herself in the cadence of his voice. Her hunger-panged stomach dropped like she was on a roller coaster.

"Awwww. Kate is star struck." Ken's arm was suddenly around her shoulder as she sucked in her gut and begged her knees not to buckle. "Can I get you a beer, man? I brought Guinness."

"Now you're singing the song of my people."

"Cake!" Kate said loudly, hating how random the word sounded as it left her lips and echoed through the room. "Did anyone bring a cake?"

Leila

"Is anyone home?" Wes called into Ellie's living room while Leila wished the guard a good night.

"Happy Birthday!" Norah and Kate shouted in garbled unity from the stairs.

"You guys are too sweet!" Her heart swelled at the banner hanging beneath them that was too unique not to be Kate's handiwork.

"Happy Birthday, beautiful." Wes kissed her cheek and she ducked her head into his warmth for a moment, both flattered and embarrassed that they had gone to so much trouble.

"Thank you." She was about to say she wished she'd put more thought into her outfit when the sight of Pat Grayson on the landing made her do a double-take.

"And Pat's here?" She clasped her hands together and a tear sprang from her eye when she saw Ellie's grin.

"In the flesh." He raised his cane.

"You should sit down," Leila said, immediately regretting the words. "I mean if you want to. Unless you've been sitting on a plane all day. Of course you have. What am I thinking? I am just so happy to see you guys. I can't believe you did all of this just for me."

"I actually arrived last night. You're considerate to think of me though. It's no surprise my mum liked you so much."

He maneuvered to the next step and patted Ellie's hand as if to reassure her he wouldn't fall. Leila looked away, certain that if she were in his shoes she wouldn't want an audience watching her descent.

"Happy Birthday!" Cami emerged from the swinging kitchen doors with her favorite bottle of cabernet. "I meant to get you a card, too, but I ran out of time."

"You're here. That's more than enough!"

"Thanks. Let's go open this while we wait for the cake." Cami draped an arm around her shoulder and they walked toward the balcony.

Ellie

Outside, lilac paper lanterns and pom-poms made of crushed silver roses dangled from the pergolas as clear Edison bulbs crisscrossed back and forth from the upper deck down to the recessed space that held the hot tub, then back up again to the fire pits. Skinny tapers nestled in beach sand flickered in glass hurricanes on the marble bar of the outdoor kitchen and bunches of white Gerbera daisies tied with rosemary accented the side tables next to the chairs.

"This is above and beyond. Thank you all so much." Leila flushed at the sight of her favorite flowers.

"It was all Wes," Ellie laughed, kissing her cheek and giving Wes a nod of thanks as he pulled out the barstools beside his wife for her and Pat.

"With a little help from your friends," Wes chuckled.

"True story," Cami grunted, readjusting the wine bottle sandwiched between her knees and pulling on the corkscrew.

"Can I, err, help you with that?" Pat asked, pausing before taking his seat.

Ellie cringed. If the introduction she dreaded most was a puddle of kerosene, Pat had just thrown in a match.

"Oh, I'm quite capable." Cami ripped half of the cork from the bottle and glared at the yellowed shards peeking out above the lip.

"And that is why Cami is a vodka girl and why I, the lover of vino, wear pants three sizes larger than she does." Leila giggled nervously. "For the record, I also think nothing of a little cork in my wine. Thanks for opening it."

"You're welcome." Cami sat the bottle and corkscrew in front of Wes. "I'm going to go find Kate and make her a plate."

"I think that went well." Pat kissed Ellie's shoulder with a sheepish grin and a wordless *I'm sorry.*

"She'll come around." Wes angled the rest of the cork out of the bottle and poured three glasses. "It may take the better part of a decade, but she will." He laughed and passed the fuller two of the three glasses to Leila and Ellie. "Leila and I simply couldn't be happier for you two."

"To beautiful evenings spent with friends," Ellie toasted.

"And to never forgetting what a blessing it is to see your next birthday," Pat finished, clinking his can of Guinness against their glasses, and impressing Ellie once again with the authenticity he so effortlessly brought to everything he did.

Norah

"Apologies." Norah covered her third yawn. "It's was a fourteen hour day before nine AM."

"I can relate to those hours." Zac lifted the second tier of coconut cake from its pink box and secured it on the supports. "I spend most of my time at the flagship café because it's the busiest, but I pop in to the two franchises at either lunch or breakfast each day. Neither is completely independent yet, and likely never will be at this rate."

He smoothed the disturbed icing around the base and angled the cake on the buffet between the platters of cheese and vegetables.

"It was kind of you to do this last minute," Norah said as he brushed a crumb of icing that had fallen onto the counter into his hand.

"I'd do anything for Cami."

Heat climbed into his cheeks and Norah hoped Cami knew what she was giving up.

Kate

"Happy now?" Kate threw her half-empty plate into the trashcan behind the outside kitchen.

"Thrilled," said Cami.

"Just don't push me. Okay? I'm doing my best. I have a lot on my mind right now."

"I know you do, but passing out on the stairs won't help any of it."

"So I like Pat Grayson more than you do and got a little flustered. No biggie. Just try and be nice to him for Ellie's sake."

"This *is* me being nice." She popped a lime into a glass of Perrier and took a sip.

"Then try harder. Let's go thank Zac for bringing the cake."

"Lead the way," Cami said as a bout of loud laughter roared from the deck below.

Ken stood in the middle of the Adirondack chairs that surrounded the fire pit regaling Wes, Pat, Zac, Ellie, Leila, and Norah with some tale involving a drunken priest at the Kentucky Derby.

"And so my mother, who is usually as quiet as a church mouse unless she has a few mint juleps in her, balls up her fists and says to my father, 'Well, Ken, now that I have seen the biggest horse's ass at the Derby, you can take me home.'"

Wes slapped his knee and let loose the loudest laugh in the group.

"There you are, Cami! Zac's here! Come sit!" Leila patted the arm of the empty seat between her and Zac, leaving Kate wishing she had remembered to tell her Cami had ended things with him.

"I'm fine," Cami said.

Pat worked his way to standing from the deep seat of the slanted Adirondack chair.

"Here you are. Take my seat. I was just about to fetch another Guinness. Can I tempt anyone else?"

"I'll join you." Zac stood with a nod to Kate. The remaining five looked anywhere else except at Cami as their conversation jarringly shifted to the unseasonably wet weather.

Ellie

Wes and Leila shared one of the overstuffed chairs flanking the sofa where Ellie, Pat, and Ken were sitting. Norah half-sat, half-stood against the arm rest and Cami had taken up post near the balcony door, as far away from Zac's seat by the fireplace as possible.

"It feels as much like a homecoming as it does a birthday," Ellie whispered to Pat, happy that some of the people she loved most in the world were perched around her living room, laughing and picking at giant pieces of cake.

"Present time!" Kate sang from the kitchen doorway holding a wicker basket on her hip.

"After all of this? You really shouldn't have."

"The first one is from Norah." Kate handed Leila the bouquet of candy bars tied with colorful curled ribbons.

"It's not much, but I'll treat you to lunch one day next week."

"Heath bars are my favorite. Thank you."

"And this is from Ken, Liam, and me."

Kate sat a lavender box tied with a densely layered silver bow onto Leila's lap. Leila raised the edges of the ribbon carefully, trying not to tear it, and slipped the lid from the box. She gasped and gingerly lifted a snow globe from the tissue paper beneath.

"I know it's early, but I wanted you to have it before you decorated for Christmas."

"Is that?"

"Yes! It's your Christmas card from last year. I had it made in January."

"This means so much to me, Kate."

"I know." Kate lowered her eyes and the poignant pause stretching between them told Ellie the snow globe was far more than unique holiday decor. "You're welcome."

"It's a really thoughtful gift, Kate." Wes planted a kiss on his wife's cheek.

"For the record, I'm sipping Cami's gift and wearing Wes' present. You all have made me feel beyond loved today."

"I'm afraid there's one more." Pat winked at Ellie and pushed himself to standing with more contortion than she liked to see. "I'll preface by saying there's no need to accept it if it makes you, or Wes, uncomfortable in any way a 'tall."

Leila blushed and Wes cocked his head, confused at what Pat was implying.

"Ellie and I owe you a great debt, both for accompanying her to New York and for being a solace to my mum."

He pulled an oblong golden envelope from his jacket pocket and handed it to her. Ellie watched the anticipation build in Leila's cautious smile as she worked a finger through the embossed red wax seal.

"You see, it would be an honor if you would accompany me to the Golden Globes' Banquet."

Leila's hand began to shake as her eyes bounced from Pat to Wes to Ellie, who chuckled that she had never seen her most talkative friend silent for so long.

"Say yes, Leila." Ellie stood and looped her arm around Pat's waist. "It's as much a gift for me as it is for you."

"Why aren't you taking Ellie?" Wes asked with his head still cocked.

"Publicists and agents aren't allowed. I wasn't going to go, but she wore me down."

"I did. The Globe's board isn't an enemy he needs to make. The *Life of Us* family agrees."

"And my condition was that I would go only if I could bring attention to a platform that is important to me instead of merely smiling and nodding while their ridiculous rule excludes my love and makes a mockery of the film I am representing."

"We chose you, Leila, because we want to say thank you for what you've done for us and because you're an outspoken advocate for outreach in education."

"We're going to auction off his shirt for The Trevor Project afterward and I thought we could do the same with his tie for Faces of Poverty. Signed by every guest willing, of course."

"Just say yes. It's a once-in-a-lifetime experience and a chance to give a nod to people everywhere living love as a verb."

"I'm flattered, to say the least, but it's so soon. What would I even wear?"

"We can take care of that. I've already made the call."

"The things these two get me into." Leila's grin threatened to fracture her face as she snuggled closer to Wes.

Leila

"**W**hat did you, Dominic, and Pat talk about out on the deck while I helped Ellie and Kate pack up the food?" Leila stroked Wes's knee as he exited the freeway.

"The Globes banquet. I think it would be a great experience for you, but..."

"But what?"

"I wanted to make sure the proper security was in place given the last time he walked a carpet. He said it's all been arranged."

"Knowing Ellie, we will probably arrive in a full blown tank."

"True. I also asked if we should worry about the girls. If these Holy Pearls people were extreme enough to plant a fake cancer patient on the red carpet as bait for an assassination, who knows what else they are capable of."

"I hadn't considered that." Her heart leapt into her throat. "Their school is on permanent lockdown, but I don't want to go if you think it will put us or them at risk."

"Dominic doesn't. He said to keep them home the day after the event, or have the school arrange for an extra patrol, and that any attention should die quickly. He also suggested a campus officer escort you to and from your car for the week after. His concern is minimal, but emphasized that we don't want to underestimate the Holy Pearls."

"Agreed." She stared out at the skyline whirring past her window, lost in thoughts of how any group anointed in hate could remotely claim to be angels of the Lord.

"But, beautiful, I want you to go. If Pat can step out on a sidewalk again, much less a red carpet, in the face of their fear tactics, the least we can do is not cower under the masses' momentary interest in our lives."

"Surely they wouldn't target him twice, especially this close to the trial. Right?"

"Who knows how people that lost in hate think." He flicked the car's navigation screen from map view to traffic view and weaved his way to the next exit while Leila compiled her own list of security questions for Ellie and Dominic.

Kate

Kate sat up straighter and rerolled the hem of her skinny jeans over her suede bootie for the fourth time. She felt like she was on a first date, not having coffee with a potential new friend while their babies played in the petri dish known as Gymboree.

"That sounds fun." Kate freed Liam's leg from the crack between the royal blue mats.

"Not as much fun as your night!" Rebecca reached into the crevice and retrieved Liam's sock. "I saw you on Pat Grayson's Instagram. Whose birthday was it?"

"It was my friend Leila's surprise party."

"I immediately snooped on your feed and saw all of the decorations you made! Can we say Pinterest-worthy?"

"Thanks." Kate busied herself wrangling Liam's foot back into his sock unable to accept a compliment on the work she was proud of. "I haven't exactly been sleeping lately, so I threw it all together with a hot glue gun and some craft store cast-offs during my bouts of insomnia."

"Well, they looked fantastic. Why aren't you sleeping?"

"Too many reasons and not enough minutes to tell you before I have to take Liam home for his nap."

"I have a full pack of puffs to delay the baby clock and two willing ears. You should know that I want this to be a real friendship. I want us to be able to talk about the hard stuff together, almost like we are in a mini-meeting we can take our kids to."

Rebecca's pleading eyes and Kate's need for an impartial ear outweighed her nerves and, knowing almost nothing about this woman beyond their shared disease, she spilled her stress— the pregnancy test, her three-day fast, the party—rounding it all out with her resentment that Leila was the one going to the Golden Globes' banquet when she had done so much more than simply stock Ellie's refrigerator.

1 Week Later

Leila

oly Super-Spanx, Batman, Leila thought as she stood in the three-way mirror, looking at least thirteen pounds lighter and wearing a royal blue Christian Siriano party dress. She took out her phone and sent a quick picture to Ellie.

"Step up here if you are ready, Mrs. Oliver, and we will make you perfect," Meredith, the seamstress said, sitting on the bottom rung of a stepstool and gesturing to the platform in the middle of the mirrors.

"Of course."

Leila smiled, hoping she didn't need to explain that this wasn't something she did every day, as pin after pin fine-tuned what she had considered a perfect fit just moments ago into the most flattering thing she had ever worn, including her wedding dress.

Cami

"I'm not saying it wasn't *nice* of you to bring the cake; I'm saying I didn't expect you to stick around for the rest of the night."

Cami followed Zac through the swinging door into the café's kitchen.

"And here I thought you were actually inviting me to the party." Zac raised his voice over the din of the line cooks furiously chopping vegetables and searing chicken breasts for the evening's menu.

"Well, I didn't. I asked if you had any nice cakes in the bakery that could be delivered on short notice. I intended to pay for it."

"Understood." His shoulders fell and his eyes bored into hers like he was looking straight through her.

"It's not that I minded you being there. It's just..."

"It made you think of us as a couple because all of your friends were paired up and that's not something you're open to. I get it. I'm the guy who brings you cake in the middle of my restaurant's rush hour, then doesn't hear from you for a week, and the guy you sleep with when you're sad. I'm nothing more to you than a convenience."

"Zac—"

"Don't worry. I won't be chasing you."

He wiped his hands on his apron and Cami stared into everything she didn't want and hadn't meant to hurt.

Norah

"Cabo? As in San Lucas?"

"Why not? We can take a charter plane Friday evening and be eating huevos rancheros Saturday morning. We'll come home late Sunday afternoon. Tell me you don't want to get away from your life for a few hours."

"I believe escaping from our lives is what got us into this mess in the first place," Norah said as Enrique spread cream cheese over his room service bagel. "And what about Deanna? Do we really want to fan to that fire? Every time the mail comes, I am terrified there will be a letter from the ethics committee or worse."

"She's not going to sue you, Norah."

"How can you be so sure?"

"Because I agreed to give her everything she wants in the divorce, down to my golf clubs, if she promised not to. It's settled. As for the ethics committee, you followed procedure and *if* they get wind of it, which they won't now that she gets to keep eighty percent of our savings, it will be an open and shut case."

"You didn't have to do that."

"I did it for you. All I want is my freedom and time with my children. So, what do you say? We're already paying for our sins, so why not have some fun in the sun?"

"All right," she caved, not remembering the last time she had had so little to lose.

Ellie

"I don't know how I feel about sending you off with another woman looking this good." Ellie pivoted on her tiptoes and scissored Pat's freshly trimmed hair between her fingers.

"I could always stay here with you."

"Not a chance."

"Are you sure?" He took her lips in his and spread his fingers over her lower back. "We could spend the rest of the day in bed and overexert me."

"Mmmm...tempting, but you're not getting out of this that easily."

"Tonight then."

He beamed and pulled at the corners of the tie she couldn't wait to take off of him.

Leila

"**M**e in heels and Pat with a cane. What could possibly go wrong?" Leila joked into the Bluetooth speaker as Ellie told them to have fun for the second time.

"I am wagering now would be the time to tell you we blew the whole thing off and had the driver whisk us over to the McDonald's instead. The food is better here," Pat laughed.

"Very funny, guys. I'm hanging up now. Post pictures. Goodbye."

In true Ellie fashion, a pause stretched over the line before she ended the call. Leila's most romantic, yet most guarded, friend never let go of anything she loved until the last possible second within her control.

"Goodness, do I love that woman," Pat said as though he was alone. He blinked at Leila. "I, err, meant to say that in my head."

"It's fine. I love her, too."

"Has anyone ever told you that you have a knack for making people feel like they've known you for years in mere minutes?"

"No, but I'll take it as a compliment." Leila smoothed her dress and said a silent prayer she wouldn't trip or embarrass herself. "Do you still get nervous at these events, or is it old hat for you now?"

"I'd like to say it's routine, but I still feel like the kid stepping out at the *Destiny* premiere every single time."

"That's because you're grateful for your success. If you took it for granted, you would sit here arrogant and not reflective on what brought you here."

"I've never thought about it that way."

"Alright," Dominic said over his shoulder. "We're next. Remind me what you're going to do, Mrs. Oliver."

"Hopefully, not fall."

"If you do, you do. I want your eyes on the back of my bald head the whole time. Smile and wave all you want, but neither one of you stops unless I do. LAPD is here, but we ain't getting any special treatment. Got it?"

"Yes sir."

Leila's hands began to tremble and she crossed them in her lap over her clutch. Dominic's door opened and closed to an avalanche of white flashing fire. As comfortable as she had felt with the 'Pat and the commoner on the carpet' angle two minutes ago, the reality that she was not only wholly out of place but also wholly exposed hit her like a ton of bricks.

"Just breathe."

Pat's door cracked and the wall of light splintered into an explosion that froze her to her seat. He reached for the handle and pulled it closed on the chorus of voices screaming his name.

"Take one solid breath and then we will go make loads of money for some deserving kids. Ready?"

His icy palm slid into hers and she let him lead her into the roar.

Norah

"*L*eila looks lovely." Evelyn, Norah's mother, exclaimed as they watched her step out of the car holding Patrick Grayson's hand, then take his offered arm. Leila had made them promise not to let the girls watch live just in case something catastrophic happened.

"It's Mommy!" Clara pointed at the screen.

"She looks like a *pincess*." Julia proclaimed from Norah's lap.

"The Golden Globes' banquet is as much a tradition as the awards itself," said a reporter on the screen. "Today, we will see the nominees and their guests gather in an agent- and publicist-free zone. This, ladies and gentlemen, is the room where it happens. Collaborations will begin, bringing who knows what genius to the screen."

The camera panned in on Pat and Leila, showing a close up of the hand on his cane.

"Yes, indeed. It may be a long-held tradition in Hollywood, but our next guest was in a unique scenario."

His voice faded as the sound feed cut to a reporter on the carpet.

"Pat Grayson! Welcome! It's good to see you on your feet!"

"Thank you." Pat smiled into the lens and Leila, having stopped a beat too late, took an awkward step back.

"Would you like to introduce us to your date?"

"This lovely lady is Mrs. Leila Oliver, a highly decorated teacher and close mate of Ellison Lindsay."

"And where is Ellison today?"

"Watching from her office I suppose. Wouldn't it be nice if she were allowed to be here?"

"Ah, yes. I hear you were in quite the dilemma. Will we be seeing her at the awards ceremony tomorrow night?"

"She wouldn't miss it." He seamlessly segued into the money he and Leila hoped to raise for The Trevor Project and The Faces of Poverty.

"Where did Mommy and the prince go?"

"Inside to the ball!" Evelyn stood and clapped her hands. "That means it's time for our tea party! Your mommy left us scones and a very special tea set!"

Clara scrambled up from the carpet. "Is it the fancy flower cups with the really real saucers and the really real handles?"

"That's right!"

"Yea! Come on, Sister!"

"Go wash your hands and we'll get started!" Norah watched them race down the hall to their bathroom. "You are going to be a wonderful grandmother, mom."

"Thank you. I can't wait to do things like this with your child."

"He or she will be lucky to have you."

"Just as we were lucky to have Gran. I am glad she's not in pain anymore, but I still miss her every day."

"Me, too." Norah put her arm around her mother, understanding new dimensions of their bond with each day her own baby grew.

Leila

"And here is the selfie we took in the car."
Leila flipped through the pictures on her phone and rested her cheek on Wes's shoulder.

"And this one was at the table. Pat posted it and it was, no exaggeration, at one million likes before I even got a filter on mine. He tagged Faces of Poverty every time and our following exploded. I can't wait to see what happens to our outreach this year."

"That's amazing, beautiful." Wes grinned down at her.

"Here's a picture of the place card with my name on it. I think those are flecks of actual gold in the ink. It's in my purse."

"You took it?"

"Pat did." She kissed his cheek before chattering on. "I was too embarrassed to grab it when we left. Oh, and this one was of the seafood tower. Can you believe the size of those prawns? Don't worry, everyone was taking tons of pictures of the tablescape so I didn't look too astronomically out of place."

"If this is the spread for the scholarships and smaller honors, imagine what Ellie is in store for tomorrow night." Wes smoothed her hair behind her ear.

"I can't wait to watch. I think I'll invite the girls over. Ellie gave me a sneak peak of her dress and it is gorgeous."

"I bet it doesn't hold a candle to this one." He rubbed the back of her neck with his thumb and forefinger.

"Right there." Leila adjusted his hand a quarter-inch to the left, where her latest stress knot had taken up residence. "And then I'll let you take it off of me."

Ellie

Ellie studied her reflection in a tri-fold mirror of the suite she had reserved at the Beverly Wilshire.

"It matches your skin tone to perfection, Ms. Lindsay!"

Her long-time stylist, Miguel, clapped his hands as his dresser laced the corseted back of the blush colored gown.

"There must be a hundred yards of beaded tulle here," the make up artist commented, dotting a highlighting powder over her collarbone and across the dip of her trussed up cleavage.

Two gilded straps, no wider than strands of piano wire, held the flowing fabric over her shoulders as the tight bodice melded to her torso before falling into shimmering sheer folds that angled one after another to skim the floor.

"It's stunning."

"It takes a special client to pull off something this subtle," Miguel said. "The lighting will make it a sheer pink and a solid neutral all at once. My award looks are like children to me. I will never admit I have favorites, but if I did, it would be this one."

Ellie's assistant stepped into the room. "Ms. Lindsay? Mr. Grayson has arrived."

"Tell me you meant to say his car has arrived?" Ellie found her eyes in the mirror. "As we discussed?"

"No ma'am. He's in the master sitting area. He, um, didn't follow instructions."

"Please tell him my life would be a lot easier if he would drop the gentleman act."

Ellie sighed and the assistant backed quickly out of the room.

"Ah, come on, Ellison." Miguel lifted the layers of freshly colored hair that swept down her left shoulder from an off-center, tightly pinned, chignon to spray a mystery ingredient on the clear strap.

"He has to walk on that cane all night with the world watching. He should have saved his strength."

"The fact that he didn't, when no one was watching, should tell you something."

It's not an act, Ellie thought as Miguel finished the look with borrowed teardrop pearls that dangled from thin rose gold pendants and moved with her hair.

"Thank you, Miguel. Your eye is, as usual, on point."

The dress was heavier than she had anticipated and the deceptively delicate fabric swooshed across the carpet like chainmail as she thanked each member of Miguel's team and posed for selfies. Ellie took the understated peach satin clutch from the entry table by the door, checked that the necessary lip and eye touch ups were inside, and straightened into her most perfect posture before opening the door.

Pat stood with his back to her on the opposite side of the room looking at the skyline and leaning slightly on the high back of a winged chair. He turned at the sound of the door closing and it was Ellie who stopped speechless. The gleaming black fabric of his tuxedo hugged the muscles of his arms and flared perfectly over the line of his hips. Her eyes traced the delicate piping of the oyster colored shirt beneath the jacket. The intricate tailoring seemed to accentuate every ripple the months of compensating for a healing back had carved into his abdomen, rendering it into a sheath more solid than it had been since the height of his *Destiny* days. He caught her stare and she felt the heat rise into the flesh of her throat.

"You look incredible," Pat all but whispered. He took four unassisted steps forward then stopped to find his balance.

"Pat—"

She gathered the beaded skirt into the balls of her hands and moved as quickly as her shoes would let her to meet him in the middle of the room.

"In my defense, the sight of you tonight would surely send the most sure-footed man to the ground."

He placed one hand on her shoulder and cupped her cheek with the other. Ellie ran her hand into the back of his hair and pressed his forehead to hers.

"I am so glad we're here and that you're mine. I love you, Patrick Grayson."

"This is us," he whispered, "ruining your lipstick."

"I have someone to fix it."

Ellie's laugh filled the room and he kissed her until Dominic cleared his throat from an unseen corner and told them it was time to leave.

Kate

ate dipped her fifth piece of celery into her second table-
spoon of hummus, knowing Leila would politely accept her
nausea excuse and not push her any further. Thankfully,
Cami had lost interest several awards ago and was now talking Fantasy
Football with Wes in the kitchen. She scrolled through her phone and
pinned every image she could find of Pat and Ellie to the secret Pinterest
board she had cheekily titled 'PatSon at The Globes.'

Ellie had looked ethereal floating down the red carpet on Pat's arm.
They had been first to arrive and stopped at every single microphone on
the way inside, expressing their gratitude to the fans supporting them
and charging each and every one to be a light, not only against the out-
right darkness of organizations like the Holy Pearls, but against smaller
shadows in their everyday lives, like schoolyard bullies and misogynistic
colleagues. In a touching show of unity, each celebrity who arrived after
Pat and Ellie exited their cars using canes with the phrase *Love Wins. Always.*
engraved into the handles and autographed their tributes on camera to
be donated to the Trevor Project.

"This is it!" Leila said as the last clip ended and Neil Patrick Harris
recapped the nominees for Best Actor.

"And the Golden Globe goes to..." he paused and a visible tear sprang to his lashes. "Patrick Grayson for *Life of Us*!"

Neil rubbed his shoulder to his eye and tucked the envelope beneath his arm to join in the audience's wild applause.

Ellie

E llie pushed the breath she'd been holding from her lungs and threw her arms around Pat, kissing him then drawing back to cup his face, unaware for a millisecond that the world was watching them. The width of his grin met his eyes and he pushed himself up from his seat more quickly than his fatigued back could tolerate, turning red as he fell awkwardly into the armrest.

"It's okay. Here."

She wedged her arm beneath his weaker side. They stood together and she held his cane until he was steady. His eyes were full of an emotion she could best file between gratitude and adoration as the *Life of Us* theme, Michael Bublé's cover of *I Just Can't Help Falling in Love with You*, began to play. Arms from the table behind them circled her and applause roared louder with each step Pat took to the stage. The bartenders in the back of the room began to chant "Love Wins!" and the raucous noise frothed into a boil as Neil clasped Pat in a tight hug and handed him the award.

"What's that? I'm out of time?" Pat said to an imaginary person in the wings and the audience laughed. "In all seriousness, I stand, as loosely as that term applies to my present mobility, here in front of you a changed man. I would like to thank my brilliant director both for taking a chance on a dying man's love legacy and for trusting me to portray it. This award is for lovers everywhere and dedicated to Roland and Mark. The film ends with Roland's charge to his widower and their children. He says 'Maybe only one of your love stories can end in happily ever after. When you find it, don't waste a minute not writing it.' I've had a lot of time to reflect on these words that were said as a last wish of sorts to the people he held dearest, and, while I wish its truth hadn't—quite literally—been shot into me, I have chosen to live his words. You see, I've had a lot of love stories."

Pat paused and a titter of nervous laughter rippled through the crowd.

"It's okay," he grinned and pushed his hand through his hair. "She already knows."

They laughed again and Ellie gave a knowing smile into the camera that would broadcast her reaction worldwide.

"The hate that was meant to either end my life or sentence me to a closeted existence has instead given me a gift. It has given me an indomitable woman named Ellison Lindsay and thrust our budding relationship into a white-hot trial by fire. We've lived love's most delightful highs and most demanding lows in the course of mere days. In fact, this is essentially our fourth proper date. How'd I do, love?"

Pat held for the applause and tugged at his tie. Ellie shifted in her seat at the mischievous glimmer in his eyes.

"And considering we've logged a helluva lot of living in between what the world has seen and what they haven't, I would like to ask you a question."

Pat sat the statue on the podium and dropped painfully to one knee producing a blue diamond ring from his jacket.

"This is me asking you to balter with me through what we can't control for the rest of my tomorrows."

The room erupted into a chorus of squeals and cheers, then quieted instantly as the utter wordless shock on Ellie's face and a shake of her head filled airwaves around the world with her *no*.

Continued in The Circus of Women Trilogy, Volume III. To unlock an excerpt now, visit www.NicoleWaggonerAuthor.com.

Acknowledgments

First and foremost, I want to thank my husband, Mike, for being my unwavering champion. He would like you all to know that he knows how this story ends and can be bought. Thank you to Noah and Maya. You are my heartstrings and I love you to the moon and back. I have solid faith that you will make our world a better place. Love always wins and happy hearts can't lose.

I want to thank every single reader who invited my imaginary friends into their lives. You are the reasons I keep rambling. Thank you, infinity, to my "Circus of Women" squad. You know who you are and I could do none of this without you. I wish I had five hundred pages to name you all, but, alas, I do not. Regardless if you're listed or not, please know you are loved. More acknowledgments to come in future works! In particular, I would like to thank Susan Peterson, Letty Blanchard, Nita Haddad, Cindy Burnett, Jennifer Morgan, Jen Cannon, Lori Parker, Jill LeVan, Kendra Breithaupt, Candice Vinson, Suzy Pruka, Nancy Sherod, Andrea Bates, Kelli Attkinson, Paige Templeton, Suzanne Fine, Heather Walker Shin, Suzan Roberts, Sasha Clements, Grace Johnson, Sherri Nichols, April Huff, Claudia Swisher, Joy Potter, Tonni Callan, Deborah Blanchard, Rebecca Hill, Cyndi Stumpf, Kathy Lewison, Brea Clark, Hailey Fish, Jill Hughes, Melissa Seng, Misti Connelly, Jaymi Couch, and Denise Stout Holcomb.

I have often said that releasing a book is akin to sending a naked selfie out into the world. That said, book communities and those who facilitate beautiful spaces for book lovers to gather have a special place in my heart. Thank you, Andrea Katz, for creating Great Thoughts

Great Readers. I would like to give special thanks to Melissa Amster, who I know caught every single *Hamilton* allusion; to Jenny O'Reagan, who shares my ardent love of literacy outreach and sun protection; to Kayleigh Wilkes, who understands the stresses of this season; to Kristy "Bee" Barrett, who gives more than she receives; to Barbara Kahn, who makes me want to live in her suitcase; to Caryn Strean, who is a book whisperer; to Courtney Marzilli, who keeps my makeup bag as full as my TBR; to Lauren Margolin, who is a good fairy indeed; to Mrs. Mommy Booknerd, who juggles it all; to Kathy Murphy, who earned that tiara and pays it forward; and to Robin Homonoff, who brightens as many authors' lives as she does smiles.

Thank you to Coach Sherri Coale for inspiring me from the moment we met and for cultivating extraordinary young leaders on the court and in the classroom. Cami's crack that there are 'no hustle points in golf' is for you. To Kenna Treece, I'll always be in your court. Phenomenal young women like you make me feel better about sending my children out into the world.

Finally, I would like to express my gratitude to my fellow writers for welcoming me to the table. Again, I wish I had room to name everyone who has been kind to me. Thank you to the women of WFWA for your wisdom, your guidance, and your unwavering faith in the scribble. Thank you to the Tall Poppy Writers for supporting Room to Read as much as your fellow blooms. Thank you to Liz Fenton and Lisa Steinke for the laughs-we all want to be your BFFs! Thank you to Lisa Barr and Camille Di Maio for being role models on and off of the page. To Katie Moretti, Jaime Ford, Kerry Lonsdale, Stephanie Evanovich, Orly Lopez, Pam Jenoff, Cristina Alger, Susie Orman Schnall, Scott Wilbanks, Kristy Woodson Harvey, Caroline Leavitt, Ellen Urbani, Diane Haeger, Jaime Brenner, Kaira Rouda, Emily Liebert, Allyson Richman, Aimie Runyan, Jaime Raintree, Laura Drake, Susie Orman Schnall, Karma Brown, Whitney Dineen, and Ann Wertz Garvin, it has been my pleasure to get to know you IRL, as the kids say, on social media, or, in many cases, in both.